# HALLOWEEN HAUNTS
## An Anthology of Horror Stories

# Edited by Dorothy Davies

# HALLOWEEN HAUNTS
## An Anthology of Horror Stories

GRAVESTONE PRESS

# CONTENTS

# CONTENTS

# The Dissectionist
## Lena Ng

The room was cool, the fire burning low in the hearth, with a bare concrete floor and bare plaster walls. The acrid smell of formaldehyde. The rolling trolley. His tools shiny, sharpened, laid out on the workman's bench: a handsaw, scalpels of various sizes, forceps, scissors. The dissectionist, burley and broad, wearing his leather apron, stood at the width of the body table. The *skritch* of the knives.

A loose arm hung over the table's edge, anticipating, only slightly mottled, the red of the veins chilled into blue, like delicate branches on a dead tree. The skin was cold, icing into rigidity, grey; the eyes earth brown, muddy and opaque.

The corpse monger stood at the door frame, waiting for his coin. "Fresh from the garden," he said. "Poor one, planted only yesterday. Unnamed, in an unmarked grave. No one will miss him."

"That's what you said last time." The dissectionist's graveyard voice could make any man's skin crawl.

The corpse monger shrugged. "Should have guessed he had a long-lost cousin. They come out of the woodwork at the smell of money." He shifted his weight from leg to leg. The night waned and there would be more bodies to be gained if he were on his way.

The dissectionist scrutinized the body with an expert eye. It was a nice specimen. No visible injuries, despite the pool of blood settling on the

7

back. No outward deformities, although they would make good teaching examples for the medical students. The linen shroud had kept the insects at bay.

He reached into a pocket and counted some coins. "A discount from last time. And next time, I want a woman. I'll pay a premium for one." The money exchanged hands.

The corpse monger accepted the payment with a curdled expression, but made no argument. The last body had put both their livelihoods at risk. The dissectionist was also a dependable customer with whom he'd done much business over the years. He grumbled under his breath and disappeared back into the night.

The dissectionist began with a broad cut down the length of the body, beginning at the neck, and ending down the full length of the torso. He slowly cut away the five major organs—the lungs, liver, kidneys, brain (after a short time sawing into the skull), and heart—from the connective tissue, preserving segments of the highways of veins and arteries routing into the structure, before placing each into a jar of preserving fluid. He worked down from the major organs to the smaller ones—such as the pancreas and gallbladder—until all seventy-eight organs rested in glass. Hours passed and the darkness of night gave way to the grey of early morning. The labelling and routing of the jars would be the next night's work, along with the preparation of the skeleton. The dissectionist removed his leather apron, put out the fire, washed his hands, and locked up.

8

The dissectionist trudged home through the empty streets, then through the dew-dampened fields to his lonely cottage. The interior was gloomy. No wood burning in the fireplace. No warm woman with a smile of welcome. Usually, he enjoyed the quiet solitude, but today for some reason, it felt empty. Some corner of his heart ached. He made himself a humble meal of cheese and stale bread, washed down with a mug of watery ale. Afterwards, he curled onto a cot and fell into sleep.

*\*\**

This one was a beauty. Thick waves of mahogany hair. Unmarked skin like parchment. Thin from the ravages of consumption. Dead eyes, of course, but the colour of a stormy sea.

The corpse monger's liver-coloured lips stretched out in glee. "A nice one, no? Saved it especially for you. What do you think?"

The dissectionist stood as though stunned into silence. Her beauty, so fleeting, must be preserved. As promised, he paid the corpse monger double as premium. With his morbid smile lingering, the corpse monger went on his way.

The organs were small and slight, the lungs black from disease. The dissectionist removed all but the heart, which he left nestled in the body, and the eyes which he injected with formaldehyde. The empty cavity of her torso, he filled with sawdust and wood shavings.

He opened a trapdoor in the corner of the workhouse, gathered the body and carried her down the creaking stairs. He wrapped her in linen and placed her in a sand-filled coffin, covering her remains. He had tinkered with the ventilation of the room and hoped this time the drying process would take and her body would preserve.

He waited four weeks before checking back on the body. The results were beyond what he thought could be believed. She looked almost the same as the day he had received her, though there was some gauntness to the cheeks, some thinning of the lips. The linen shroud and internal sand had absorbed the body fluids which would have led to decay. It was now time to take her home.

\*\*\*

She was so small, she could be folded into a duffle bag. He carried her body back to his home. The clothes he chose for her were too large; his first wife was big-boned and full-fleshed and had sewed their clothing with care and he had a full wardrobe for his new bride's needs. He propped her in a chair as he ate his meal. Afterward it felt strange, since it had been three years, to have another body in the bed. He smelled her hair as he wrapped his arms around her and his breath deepened into dreams.

In his dream, his new bride was dressed in her white wedding gown. He bowed and she curtsied. In the otherwise empty ballroom, they began a wedding waltz. The room spun around and around.

Their feet left the floor and they danced like marionettes in mid-air, as though in an invisible music box. He ignored the shadows in the corners.

When evening came, before he left for work, he picked flowers from the garden, large rose blooms he placed on his new wife's lap. His first wife's body had well-fertilized the land. It was an accident, he assured himself. He didn't mean to. He would ensure he would treat this new wife with more care. This wife at least would be silent, which would lead to no arguments. His dormant heart awoke into joy.

\*\*\*

The dissectionist whistled as he worked on the body. The corpse monger was strangely amused. "Never seen a man enjoy his work so much," he said. "Especially the work that it is."

The dissectionist shrugged a shoulder. He now looked forward to the end of the night, to go home to an agreeable soul to whom he could unburden his problems, to a beautiful face who would worship him in silence.

The body brought to him was another woman, though her face was weathered and worn as lived outdoors. A scarf was gathered around her head, and rings of silver hung from her ears. She looked suspiciously fresh and didn't smell of the grave.

He gave an inquisitive glance at the corpse monger. "Don't ask," the corpse monger said. "Though she won't be missed, for she was a wanderer."

11

After the corpse monger departed, he undressed the body, feeding the clothes to the fire. He put the jewelry aside. The rings of silver from ears and fingers. The thin bangles. The necklace with the heart-shaped locket, the inscription within reading "Love never dies."

He lost track of time as he went about his dark work. A darting movement in the corner of his eye. The swoop of a bat as it flew across the room, chasing the insects which had been attracted by the fire. He took a cloth and waved it at the intruder. He rushed from one corner of the room to the other, trying to drive the bat back into the night. His foot caught on the unevenness of the floor, he tripped, and slammed his right cheek on the edge of the table.

After a few days, the swelling had gone down but the shooting, stabbing pain remained. Nerve damage, the alley doctor had said. He had been prescribed a course of leeches, a minor blood-letting, and a tincture of opium to numb the pain that shot down his cheek to his jaw and onward to his teeth. Although it helped, over the next few months, the doctor turned stingy with the prescriptions and with ever mounting bills, he turned to the opium dens for relief.

When the dissectionist emerged from one of these dens, he left in a cloud of haze into the chill of autumn. Tonight was the Feast of All Saints, the night where there was a blurring between the living and dead, the night when the living could dance with the dead. The opium dulled the pain, but his face still throbbed with a pulsing ache. The wind swept in from the graveyard and gave him a chill. The shadows seemed to dance and he didn't know what was real and what was only a vision.

At home, this time, his new wife didn't wait passively to greet him. Her hair was put up in ringlets and she wore her finest satin gown the blush-pink of new roses. The necklace he had gifted her glinted in the gloom. "Love never dies" it read, and it seemed she had awakened. She curtsied, and surprised, he bowed. She put her cold hands in his, and silently they waltzed throughout the room, the hem of her gown with a quiet swish against the floor. Her heart, the only organ she had in her body remaining, seemed to beat in time to the silent music. She lowered her head to his neck. Despite the coursing of blood, his love for her blotted out the pain of her bites.

# The Congress of Familiars
## David Turnbull

There was a dog barking in the night.

It was twenty past ten on Halloween. Andy lay in bed, still buzzing from the night's sugar rush. His zombie costume, an old school uniform dusted in flour and speckled with ink to look like mildew, hung on his wardrobe door like a dead man's skin.

The bedroom window was closed against the night frost, but the barking was obvious, loud and incessant. He heard his father on the landing. "Somebody should do something about that dog."

And his mother replying. "It'll quieten down soon. Probably a cat or a fox got it riled up."

The dog didn't quieten. There was a rhythmic three - two - three pattern to its bark. *Bark-bark-bark. Bark-bark. Bark-bark-bark.* Then a momentary beat before the pattern repeated. Andy listened intently. There was no deviation from the three-two-three pattern.

If there was a fox or a cat, he thought, it would have ran off by now.

Andy tried to figure out what kind of dog it was. A little dog like a Chihuahua would have a high-pitched *yip-yip-yip*. A terrier would be more *yap-yap-yap*. It didn't sound like a German Shepherd. Andy settled on a Labrador.

He heard his mother calling from the kitchen.

"What are you doing out there? It's freezing."

His father answered from the garden. "I'm trying to figure out where the barking is coming from."

"What good does that do?"

"If I could figure out where it's coming from, I could go round there and tell them to quieten their dog."

"Maybe they're not home?" suggested Andy's mother.

The dog went through another run of the sequence.

Bark-bark-bark. Bark-bark. Bark-bark-bark.

"They shouldn't be allowed to have a dog if they've going to leave it barking like that."

"Just come inside," said his mother. "By the time we're ready for bed the dog will have settled down."

A moment later Andy heard the kitchen door shut and the sound of his parents passing along the corridor to the front room. Voices from the TV hummed up through the floorboards. *Bark-bark-bark*, went the dog out in the night. *Bark-bark. Bark-bark-bark.*

Andy indulged himself in a little fantasy.

In the fantasy his father figured out where the barking was coming from. He asked Andy to get out of bed and go round there with him. Andy's mother put some cubes of stewing steak into one of her Tupperware containers.

Andy and his father went out into the night like men on a mission. They came to the house where the dog was barking. All the windows were dark. No one was home. Andy's father climbed over the

15

fence. Andy handed him the Tupperware container and scrambled over behind him into the garden.

The dog was chained up to a doghouse with a red roof, just like the ones you see in cartoons. The dog was a Labrador, exactly as Andy had worked out. It barked its three-two-three sequence as they approached.

Andy's father handed him back the Tupperware container. Andy removed the lid and set it down before the dog. It sniffed the steak cubes. Its tail wagged joyfully as it devoured the meat. When it was done it licked its lips, barked once, as if to say thank you. Then it fell into a deep slumber.

And the night was quiet once more.

Andy thought he could probably figure out which garden of which house the dog was barking from. He closed his eyes and tried to remember which of his neighbours he'd seen out walking their dogs.

There was an Indian lady who lived down near the post office who had a cocker spaniel. And then there was Wendy Constantino from his class at school, whose parents had gotten her a labradoodle for Christmas, already big enough to have a bark that would echo in the night. Was Wendy home? Wasn't she down the precinct just the other day boasting that she was off on a city break with her parents and that they we're putting the Labradoodle in kennels? What if they forgot to drop off the dog at the kennels? That would sure stress it out enough to bark all night.

Suspect number one, thought Andy.

He tried to think if there was anyone else he'd seen with a dog. There was a guy who Andy had seen in the park dressed in some sort of delivery driver uniform. He had a bow-legged bulldog that wheezed and strained against its leash.

There was a kid called Barry Weathers in the class below him at school who was always making people laugh with stories about his big sister's Pomeranian. *It's like a hairy, overgrown hamster,* he'd say. *She carries it around in a shoulder bag and feeds it gummy bears.*

Bark-bark-bark, went the dog out in the night. Bark-bark. Bark-bark-bark.

Andy didn't think a Pomeranian could muster a bark like that. He didn't think it sounded like a spaniel, a labradoodle, or a bulldog either. He was sticking firmly to his Labrador theory. But he couldn't think of anyone he'd seen with a Labrador. His Halloween head told him that it could be a ghost, or a ghoul, or a vampire making the dog bark. But his father would never go for that, so he needed a sensible explanation.

Blind people used Labradors as guide dogs. Maybe a blind man had fallen down and injured himself in his garden and his guide dog was barking to call for help? Or, maybe it was a stray? A poor stray dog, barking in the night because it needed a home and a new master.

This could be its home, thought Andy, I could be its master.

He would take it for long walks down by the canal. He would take it to the park to play fetch with an old chewed up tennis ball. It would be obedient. But only to Andy. If Andy said sit his dog would sit. But if someone else said sit it would look at them with disdain as if to say, *who are you to tell me what to do?*

It wouldn't work, though. His father would never agree to a dog.

Do you know how much it costs to feed a dog? he'd say. Do you know how much vet's fee are? Do you think money grows on trees?

Andy felt suddenly let down and disappointed. As if he'd actually found a stray dog and his father had actually spoken those exact words. *He always spoils things,* thought Andy, turning on the pillow. *Even in my imagination.*

Outside the dog went on barking. *If it's a stray*, thought Andy, *the dog catcher will get it.*

Was there such a thing as a dog catcher? Or was that just in the movies?

He heard his parents talking in the corridor again.

"You're not going out there," said his mother.

"I'll just take a walk around the block and see if I can find where the barking is coming from."

"And if you find it? What then?"

"I'll knock on the door and ask politely if they could calm down their dog. There wouldn't be any sort of trouble."

"And what if no one is home?"

"I'll make a note of the address and then phone environmental health or animal welfare."

Animal welfare, thought Andy. They're bound to have a dog catcher.

"Just leave it be, would you? said Andy's mother. "I'm sure it'll stop soon."

Andy's father heaved a weary sigh. "Fair enough. It would probably be a pointless exercise anyway. It could take me all night to find it."

Andy heard his mother come lightly up the stairs. Saw the illumination fill his bedroom doorway as she went into the bathroom and switched on the light. Heard the sound of her brushing her teeth.

Bark-bark-bark, went the dog. Bark-bark. Bark-bark-bark.

Andy heard his father's heavier footfall on the stairs. They creaked a little under his weight. A moment later his father's bulky silhouette appeared in the doorway of his bedroom.

"You awake, son?"

"Yes," replied Andy.

"That damned dog, huh?"

"I could get dressed and help you try and find which house it's at," said Andy, hopefully.

"It's late," said his father.

"It's the half term holiday," Andy reminded him. "I don't have school in the morning."

"But I have work," said his father.

Just once, thought Andy. Just once when I suggest something you could say, what the hell, let's just do it."

The dog went through its three-two-three sequence.

"Damned dog," repeated Andy's father.

"Finished," called Andy's mother from the bathroom.

19

His father turned from the doorway and went to brush his teeth.

Once, a couple of summers ago, when they went on holiday to the coast, he'd had a long conversation with his mother. His father had gone to the pub and Andy was sharing a KFC bucket meal with his mother.

"How come dad never wants to do anything with me?" he asked. "I mean, today on the beach I built this excellent sandcastle. He never even looked at it. Even when I asked him. He just lay there on the sun lounger reading his newspaper. All afternoon. It was an excellent sand castle and he didn't listen when I asked him to look."

His mother's answer was like a riddle. "Your father is one of those men who was born to be a man."

Andy paused with a chicken drumstick half-way to his mouth. "What does that mean?"

"I don't think you father particularly derived any enjoyment at all from his boyhood. His memories of that time of his life are pretty hazy. His focus was entirely on becoming a man: starting to shave, putting on a suit, working on a construction site, going to a bar, talking sport and politics. That's what fired his imagination more than toys or games or such."

That made sense to Andy. His father much preferred documentaries to movies and practical books to novels. He was very fond of telling Andy he should be more grounded and not engage too much in flights of fancy, or read too many comics.

20

"He never even kicks a ball around with me like other dads do with their sons."

"Football is a perfect example," said his mother. "Your father loves his football. But for him it's serious business. It's a game for professionals, played for specific purposes, such as moving up in the league or winning the cup. I don't think he even considers it to be fun. Kicking a ball for fun would never enter his head."

Andy felt a knot twist in his gut.

"Will I be like that when I grow up?"

"Well, I certainly hope you won't be the opposite."

"What's the opposite?" asked Andy.

"A man who's born to be a child. Someone who just wants to play around all his life and never accept any responsibility for his actions."

"So, it's one or the other?"

"There's a third option," said his mother. "A man who gets the balance just about right. Someone who can be serious and responsible when that is what is necessary. But who can also be fun and frivolous when the occasion calls for it."

"I'll be that then," said Andy.

"I know you will," said his mother and mussed up his hair.

Just once, though, thought Andy now. Just once, he could say - yes, sure, let's go out and look for a dog that's barking in the night. Even if we don't find it, it'll be fun. And when we talk about it later, we'll laugh at the shared memory.

The dog was annoying him now. When he heard the light in his parents' room click off he crept out of bed and crouched low by the window. The moon was a crescent, cloaked in wispy clouds. Frost glinted on the lawn. The bamboo wind chime, hung from a branch of their little apple tree, swayed gently in the night breeze.

Bark-bark-bark, went the dog. Bark-bark. Bark-bark-bark.

"Damned dog," whispered Andy, repeating his father's words.

He looked out over the back gardens, the sheds and greenhouses, the outhouses, the lawns and the flowers beds, the patios and the decking. He could hear the dog, but he couldn't see it, or figure out which direction the barking was coming from.

All the houses in the area were terraced, joined side by side, row after row, back gardens adjoining, separated by fences and bushes erected to mark property boundaries. Someone must know where the barking was coming from. So why was no one doing anything?

Andy wondered if Luke was awake. Luke lived two doors along. He and Andy had known each other since forever. That very night they'd been trick or treating together. The inside of Luke's house was identical to Andy's. He had the same bedroom as Andy. Only he shared it with his big brother Ryan.

They had bunk beds. Ryan had the bottom bunk, because he thought it was hilarious to kick Luke's mattress to startle him when he was fast asleep in the middle of the night. Andy bet both of them were awake, wondering where the barking was coming from. Andy bet if *they* asked *their* father to take them on a night walk to go look for it, he'd say yes without hesitation.

Mr. Bedford was always doing stuff with his boys: camping, hiking, fishing, bird-watching – you name it. One Christmas holiday the three of them had played a game of Monopoly that lasted four whole days. Imagine that? A father who had the patience to play a game with his sons that lasted four whole days. Wasn't that something?

Bark-bark- bark, went the dog. I could go and find it, thought Andy. It wouldn't take long to creep through the back gardens and figure it all out. Then I could creep back in, wake up my dad, and tell him I worked it out. He wouldn't need to know I snuck out. Then we'd both go round there and quieten the damn dog down…

Mind made up, he slipped on his jeans and jumper, then some thick socks and his trainers. As an afterthought he pulled another jumper over the first so he wouldn't get too cold. Then he eased open the window, dropped down from the ledge onto the kitchen roof, scuttled crablike over the tiles and then down into the garden.

Bark-bark-bark, went the dog, as if to greet him. Bark-bark. Bark-bark- bark.

Out in the open it sounded sharper and clearer.

He felt pretty sure he knew which direction it was coming from. The frosty white lawn crunched under his footsteps. His breath billowed before him. He paused under the tinkling wind chimes and glanced over at Luke's bedroom window, just in case his friend was looking out to see where the barking was coming from. It would be great if Luke could sneak out too and join him on his dog hunt.

All he saw was closed curtains.

Bark-bark-bark, went the dog.

With a shrug of his shoulders Andy passed sideways through a gap in his garden fence into his neighbour's garden. His neighbour had a pond with half a dozen Koi. When he looked, all of the Kio has their white and gold heads upturned and partially above the surface of the icy water. They floated in eerie stillness. As if they too were disturbed by the dog.

Andy vaulted over his neighbour's wall and into the next garden. This was the last one on the row. Andy went over the next wall and found himself on the pavement, washed in the overhead glow from a tall lamppost.

The dog's incessant barking echoed from the walls of the houses.

Bark-bark-bark. Bark-bark. Bark-bark-bark.

Suddenly he knew exactly where the barking was coming from. It wasn't from a house or a back garden. It was coming from the direction of Queen Street. Andy knew what was on Queen Street. St. Saviours, the old Catholic Church. It had sat empty for years. Now it was being converted into luxury apartments. The firm his father worked for had bid for the contract, but they had been undercut.

Andy and Luke had gone there a couple of days ago and watched them remove the roof beams with a big crane. Now it was just the four outer walls. His father said there was going to be six apartments built inside those walls. His mother said hell would freeze over before she'd live in an apartment that was built inside a church.

Now there was a dog barking at the church. *A guard dog*, thought Andy. *That's what it is*. That would explain everything. His father was always talking about how thieves targeted construction sites to steal equipment and building materials. That's why they had guard dogs.

He should go home right now and tell his dad to call the police because there were thieves trying to steal stuff from the construction project at St. Saviours. He wouldn't say he'd snuck out. He'd just say he'd figured it out. And when the police arrested the thieves his dad would say - *well done, son. I'm going to listen to you more often from now on*.

But he had to be a hundred percent sure his hunch was right. The worst thing possible would be to convince his dad to send the police on a wild goose chase. He had to go there. To the church. To see the thieves with his own eyes. Then he'd be sure he was telling his dad the right thing.

Chin jutting forward he set off for Queen Street.

You could tell that it had been Halloween. Debris and detritus was scattered in its wake. Discarded candy wrappers were tumbling along the road. He walked past orange chunks of a shattered pumpkin lantern that someone had dropped. A plastic pail decorated in bats and spiders lay on its side on someone's lawn. A black balloon with a grinning skull motif was wedged in the branches of a tree. A crumpled plastic witch's mask, complete with crooked nose and pointed chin, abandoned in the gutter.

He couldn't help but crouch low as he passed along the street, convinced that one of the neighbours would draw their curtains, or bring some rubbish out to their bins, just as he was passing. Most people knew who he was and where he lived. If he was caught out on the street at this hour they were bound to haul him back home. And who knew what would happen if his dad answered the knock at the door.

Bark-bark-bark, went the dog, as if urging him on. Bark-bark. Bark-bark-bark.

Andy began to feel an apprehensive tension in his shoulders. The thieves were bound to have a van of some sort for all the equipment and materials they were planning to steal. He wished he'd thought to bring a pen and paper to write down the registration number. If he could commit it to memory that would be bound to impress his dad.

The dog carried on barking.

He could tell he was getting closer.

He noticed that he wasn't alone on the street. Ahead of him he saw a ginger cat, trotting along the middle of the road, heading the same direction as him. The cat picked up pace, moving from a trot to a gallop. Andy followed suit and broke onto a sprint, hoping the slap of his trainers against the tarmac wouldn't bring someone to their window.

He turned a corner and there were the four red stone walls of St. Saviours. A high fence of chicken wire had been erected around its grounds. *Bark-bark-bark* went the dog, so close now Andy could feel its vibrations thrum through his body. As he drew closer to the church saw there was a gap torn into the fencing. He watched as the ginger cat went slinking through.

*This must be how the thieves got in*, he told himself, and made a dash for the fence.

The fact that there was no van parked in the vicinity of the church was the first hint that his idea about thieves might be wrong. He pressed himself up to the fence and peered in. He couldn't see any shadowy figures creeping around. But he could see the barking dog. It was raised on its back haunches, sitting tall and erect by the hollow door of the church. Here too he'd gotten it wrong. It wasn't a Labrador but a hound of some sort, black shaggy hair, smattered in grey, long snout, wide ears that flopped to the sides of its head.

Bark-bark-bark, it went. Bark-bark. Bark-bark-bark.

The ginger cat trotted across the muddy churned up ground, head bowed as it passed the dog and entered the church. Moments later he saw movement close to the ground and was able to make out at least half a dozen brown field mice racing past the dog and following the ginger cat into the church.

It's calling them, thought Andy incredulously. The dog's bark is like church bells. Or like one of those Imams in a minaret, calling the faithful to prayer.

The dog stopped barking. The sudden silence pricked awkwardly at Andy's ears. The shaggy hound raised its shaggy head and sniffed the hair,

27

turning left then right. Then it fell on all fours and passed rapidly into the church.

Curiosity aroused Andy slipped through the gap in the fence. He crouched as low as he could manage, zigged-zagged from a wheelbarrow to a cement mixer and on to a pallet of bricks covered in plastic sheeting. Something dark went jittering past his eye-line. He watched it rise and realised it was a bat. It joined a host of bats, swooping and diving above the church.

This was bizarre. What was going on? Not at all what he'd expected. He had to find out.

Plastic sacks of builder's sand had been stacked up beneath the narrow slat of one of the windows. He made a dash for it, scrambled up onto the sand and looked in.

The shaggy hound was on its back haunches again, tall and upright, stationed where the priest's pulpit may once have stood. Before it was a congregation of animals, side by side: several slightly curved rows of them, one behind the other.

There were dogs of all sizes and breeds, and cats of all hues and colours. Andy could make out at least a dozen scrawny foxes, amongst just as many squirrels and rabbits and hordes of scurrying mice. There were badgers too, and hedgehogs. Creatures that by this time of year should surely be in hibernation.

Above this strange congregation brown moths fluttered in great abundance. Andy looked up to see the bats still jittering erratically above the church. Pigeons and crows were roosting on the jagged tops of the four exposed walls. Something came gliding down out of the night sky and settled amongst them in a flurry of speckled brown feather. Andy felt his mouth fall wide when he recognised it as a beady eyed barn owl.

A shiver ran through him as gooseflesh raised itself beneath every pore and hair follicle. What was it he had stumbled upon? He wished he'd paid more attention to his Halloween head. If his dad could witness this, he'd realise there was more to the world than the news and the sports pages.

In the distance came a new sound.

The town clock striking midnight.

On the last chime the shaggy hound rose on its hind legs and stood upright like a man. Andy bit his lip and covered his mouth with his hand as the creature began to swell and bloat and tremble and transform.

The floppy ears curved to a tight spiral and became ram's horns. The front legs became taut arms, outstretched fingers lacquered with vicious black claws. The hind legs on which it stood became cloven hooved goat's leg. The dog snout narrowed to a nose. Only the dog mouth remained essential the same, canine black lips over a jaw filled with horrible razor-sharp incisors.

Andy knew what this was.

It was a Halloween ritual.

Like a Christening in reverse. A Satanic baptism. Witches had animals as familiars. This was how they came to be selected.

But he was frozen to the spot up there on the pile of builder's sand, muscles locked in position, puffy breath juddering out of him. His pulse thumping so fast he felt his heart might crack his ribs. His eyes like saucers, unable somehow to do as much as blink. The demonic creature spread his arms wide and the warped shadow that fell on the church wall was like a mockery of Jesus on his cross. The eyes of the demon smouldered with an arrogant malevolence, pulsing red like ambers in a fire.

A new sound rose in the night as the animals began to pant in rhythmic unison. A cold finger traced his spine when Andy realised that their panting was like a chant, set in the same three-two-three sequence as the barking of the dog.

Huff-huff-huff. Huff-huff. Huff-huff-huff.

He saw the condensation of their breath billow forth as fingers of steam rose from their hides. The air hung heavy with the smell of damp fur, infused with the sulphurous stench of the demon. Up on the walls the pigeons cooed and the crows cawed. The bats danced a frantic aerial jig. The owl let out a solitary, ghostly hoot.

*Huff-huff-huff,* continued the unsettling chant.

Andy saw movement among the congregation. A tiny dog, no more than a bundle of brown fur on stumpy legs, was being nuzzled and nudged to the front. It bleated as it was forced forward. The panting chant grew more frenetic.

Huff-huff-huff. Huff-huff. Huff-huff-huff.

Andy had never seen a Pomeranian before but he thought it was a good guess that this was what the poor little dog was. Maybe it was *the* Pomeranian. The one that the kid always joked about. The one that was carried around in a shoulder bag and fed on gummy bears.

` A large Irish setter butted the tiny thing with its head. It rolled helplessly across the floor and came to a halt by the cloven hooves of the demon. A sharp toothed grin spread wide on the demon's leathery black lips. He clapped his clawed hands together.

A fox dashed forward and snapped at the Pomeranian, tearing off the tip of its ear. The ginger cat Andy had seen trotting along the road slashed the side of the little dog with its claws. Whimpering and bloodied, it attempted to drag itself away. More animals slunk forward to block its escape.

*A sacrificial offering*, thought Andy. To get selected as a familiar they have to show how cruel they can be.

And with those words the spell that had held him in place was broken. He ducked swiftly down from the window. He had to get away. Back through the gap in the fence. Run home as fast as his legs could carry him.

He slid down from the sacks of sand, hearing the sickening yelps of the Pomeranian being torn mercilessly to shreds. It was all too much for him. He began to cry. His only thought was to run.

No sooner had his feet touched the ground than he found his way blocked by a large, muscular Doberman. It clearly had no intention of letting him past. Head hung low, it let out a menacing growl, foam fizzing around its savage jaws. Sobbing louder now, Andy turned to see if he could find another way out. This time there were rats in his

31

way. Three of them, sleek and black, hissing through bared teeth.

Perplexed and terrified, Andy did the only thing he could think of.

"Dad!" he screamed with every ounce of air in his lungs. "Dad, I'm in big trouble! Come and get me!"

He felt a gust of air come from above him. Something hit his head so hard it almost knocked him from his feet. He glanced up to see the barn owl arcing skyward. A warm trickle of blood ran down his forehead from where the owl had raked his skull with its talons.

The Doberman lurched forward and clamped its jaws around his forearm. He felt its teeth puncture his flesh. It began dragging him toward the church doorway. *A human sacrifice would satisfy the demon more than a little lap dog*, thought Andy. His stomach cramped at the implications of the thought. To bite or claw at me would be a big step closer to becoming a familiar.

"Bring him!" roared the demon from inside the hollow church.

Andy tried to pull back but the Doberman was too strong and the pain in his arm too overwhelming. He fell to the ground, thinking his own weight might somehow slow things down. The rats came scampering up the back of his jeans. He felt their cruel little claws through the double layers of his jumpers.

"Dad!" he screamed again. "Help me, please!"

His voice echoed in the night in a manner that gave him a sliver of hope.

Somehow his hand found a crack in the wall. He wedged his fingers into it, holding on for dear life as the Doberman snarled and yanked at his other arm, praying against all the odds that for once in his life his father had heard his voice.

# Night Creeps
## Chris Rodriguez

"The power must be out in the whole area." Gabe released pent-up frustration with a hiss. "What else can happen?" He caught the sympathetic look on his wife's face in the Jeep's interior lights before they got ready to run with the kids. In this area, jack-o-lanterns were extinguished by near-freezing blustery winds. Leaves from the neighbouring trees raced noisily across the landscape, assaulting the family as they negotiated the trip from safe, warm vehicle to cold, empty house.

"See if you can find the flashlight, Coco." Gabe unbuckled the three-year-old sound asleep in his sugar-induced coma while his wife ran up the steps to unlock and prop open the front door. By the time he had Charlie up the steps and halfway down the dark hallway, Coco had scurried back out the door to get the baby. She propped the flashlight on the Jeep facing the front door to light the way. Steph was sound asleep, too. Hopefully she wouldn't wake on the way through the groaning wind into the house.

"I'll get the kids settled," Coco whispered. "You go ahead and unload just what we need until morning. The power should be back on soon. I'll grab some extra blankets."

Gabe was physically and emotionally exhausted so the suggestion of leaving the work until he'd had some rest was tempting. However, at 3:00 a.m. Halloween night, overt signs of minor vandalism in the area concerned him. His headlights coming into the subdivision had caught toilet paper streamers in neighbouring trees, broken eggs with white shells littering lawns and their own pumpkins had been smashed in the gutter in front of their house. These things were normal when porch lights were left off and no treats available for the goblin gangs scavenging door-to-door.

A nagging worry prompted him to grab the flashlight and make a quick trip around the house perimeter to make sure all was well so he could crash and burn in peace. The unplanned trip out of town for his stepfather's sudden death had been stressful for everyone, more so for him since tensions had built up in the family for years. The flat tire halfway home didn't help. The trip was a total disaster.

Things seemed to be in order, nothing obvious standing out, but his intuitive radar still raised ugly antennae of alarm. A bulky shadow passed through the flashlight beam's outer edge. Startled, he flinched and dropped it. The dim light died. *Oh, great!*

Gabe bent down, feeling the ground around him. Something ran bony fingers down his back, sending shockwaves along overstressed nerves. His imagination was magnified by his heightened senses. Numb fingers found the cold plastic of the flashlight as he turned in one swift movement toward the threat. He waited for his eyes to adjust and found only spirea branches waving in the breeze. He sighed in relief and tramped back to the Jeep. The house door was still propped open, getting even colder inside than when they arrived. He hurried to finish unloading.

A suitcase in each hand and a few items under his arms, he negotiated the steps and dropped them all on the front room floor in a pile before quickly closing the storm door, then listening for the automatic lock to click on the heavy front door. Safe inside, Gabe stood for a moment trying to adjust to his near blindness. He shook the flashlight, but the battery had given out for good. Familiar with the layout of his home, he pulled off his shoes and shuffled flatfooted down the hallway. The heat had been off for some time so the cold penetrated through the faux wood flooring, past his seasonally thick socks and into his feet. He winced. His wife would think she was sleeping with a corpse.

"Coco?" he whispered loudly. "You in bed?" She didn't answer; either asleep or buried so deep in the heavy quilts, she couldn't hear him. Feeling along the wall, he went into the bathroom to relieve his aching bladder before heading to the bedroom to snuggle with the alluring warm body of his wife.

An icicle gripped his heart. An odd chuffing sound pushed past him in the hallway coming from the direction of the bedrooms, a large form knocking him off balance in the open doorway. He heard clicking sounds like nails on the vinyl floor heading into the front room.

"What the...?" *Did somebody's dog manage to slip in through the open door?* "Hey!" he growled in a hoarse whisper. The thing stopped for only a moment before moving on. Gabe stood partially paralyzed, listening for clues. He had a powerful urge to check on his wife and kids. Just then the critter stopped. *Where is it now?* He decided to go back and open the front door to allow the animal to go back out. He felt for walls in front of him, knocking his knee on the wood chair by the door. He adjusted his direction then stood with his hand on the icy doorknob, listening for movement. None. No sound at all. No heat pump, no motors. *Damn! The refrigerator! Everything will be ruined by morning.*

Gabe opened the front door, then slowly pushed the storm door outward, sliding the tab on the bottom to hold it. He listened again, then stepped away from the door, walking carefully backward toward the hallway once more. He hoped all this activity wouldn't wake the kids. *I could sleep forever!* All was quiet, his family safe in their beds. Some relief washed over his frayed nerves. Halfway down to the rooms, he stopped. Goosebumps raised on his arms.

The chuffing sound came from the kitchen behind him, then dog's nails clicked across the front room. Gabe froze; his breath an ice block sitting heavy in his chest. He heard the storm door bang against the stair rail. *It went outside!*

Gabe hurried back down to the hall, guided by the freezing buffet of the wind coming through the front door. His eyes, adjusted to the near total blackness, could now see outside a little better. Shadows of dancing tree branches were highlighted from behind by only the lighter colored paint on some houses. He stepped out onto the stair landing and watched for movement in the night, listened for any sound from whatever had been in his home. Nothing but leaves skittering in the street. His plan successful, Gabe stepped back in to quietly close the doors.

He fastened the security chain and stood facing the door for a moment, leaning with his face against the cold paint, eyes closed in quiet repose. He was bone weary. Couldn't take another event in the long, long course of this day. Then Gabe's dark eyes opened wide in shock.

The chuffing noise next to his ear left moist, hot wetness on the back of his neck. He couldn't see but heard the sound above his own head. A pressure built in his throat. The clicking in his ear was not from the nails of a dog. The creature had not left the house. His scream never reached the chilled air.

# Halloween Dream
## Dorothy Davies

The mist swirled and moved around Dane as he huddled in the dark alleyway. It looked like ghosts, many ghosts, crowded together, peering over each other's shoulders in an effort to look at the runaway, to laugh, to point fingers and defy him to cry. He cowered against the wall, determined to be strong, not to let the ghosts intimidate him. The setting sun sent red light through the thickening mist, giving them the appearance of spooks drenched in blood. Freaky weather, he told himself, low lying mist, clear skies above, sun going down, explain it away rationally and it is not blood soaked spooks but nature at her freakiest.

It didn't help.

Dane was too young and too scared to accept any rationalisation of the phenomena; he left the alleyway and ran.

He saw without really seeing the Halloween displays in the shop windows as he passed them, pumpkins whose carved faces were far from benign, witches who snarled rather than smiled, skeletons which rattled their bones at him, white sheeted spooks which leered at him with open mouths and greedy eyes.

The mist ghosts pursued him too, laughing silently at his terror, until he hid behind a Dumpster in another alley and they stopped at the entrance, seemingly bewildered and unable to see him. It was his turn to laugh silently. Even ghosts could be outwitted, it seemed.

When it was coming up to Halloween, it was not good to be on the streets without protection. Oh yes, the monsters were supposed to wait until the 31$^{st}$, but what if they didn't? What if they thought it would be fun to creep up on people who didn't have the sense to put the barriers in place... He knew all about the things he should have; garlic, a crucifix, holy water, all of it was as remote from him as the Statue of Liberty herself – and the chance to go and visit it. No money, no shelter, no food, just another runaway on the streets, alone, scared and starving. Not in any particular order, he thought, amused at his ramblings.

'Hey, kid!'

Startled, he spun round, staring into the darkness, trying to see who had called him. A shadow moved, became larger, moved toward Dane who was absolutely petrified. The fear was so intense he felt sick.

'Hey, kid!' The shadow became a derelict, seemingly hanging in rags and dirt, half a loaf in one hand and a bottle in the other. The shabby coat he was wearing hung open, showing clothes tied up with string. 'Sorry, didn't mean to scare you. You on the run or something? Only you looked right scared when you came in - oh, this is my home, by the way.'

'Oh, really sorry.' Dane spluttered his words, trying to still his heart, to quieten the blood racing round his body. 'I didn't know.'

'Of course you didn't. How could you know? No signs are there to say this be my place.'

'I was... running from a cop.' It wouldn't do to tell the truth, that he had actually been running from the mist. It wouldn't go down very well. He was supposed to be streetwise; after all he had been out on his own now for all of two weeks – and a bit.

Trouble was he wasn't much good at it. How long did it take to become knowledgeable in the ways of runaway life? Obviously longer than that, or he wouldn't be without shelter, food and friends.

'Ah, cops. They look for young meat, so they do. Pack them off to some social officer or other and tick off another success in their quota of people they've rescued. I take it you was thieving food or something, then?'

'Sort of.'

'No need to tell me, young 'un. Been where you are a thousand times. Come with me.'

Dane had nothing to lose but his life and he felt that was not worth hanging on to these days. He followed the derelict further down the alleyway, stumbling over things which squelched as he stepped on them, touched things which were slimy and repellent when he almost lost his balance so that by the time they reached the sealed off end, he was feeling sicker than ever. Should he ask what was carpeting the alleyway? No, safer to leave it to his imagination. He had the feeling that what he would be told was worse than anything he could conjure up himself.

A dumpster had been commandeered by the derelict and used as a wall. Its wheels had

41

vanished; it sat on the ground, sturdy, solid and safe. Behind it was a lantern, flickering its warmth against the dirty walls, revealing cardboard boxes, a stained mattress, blankets, even a small stove.

'Here.' The man pushed a blanket at Dane and pointed at the mattress. 'Sit you down there, wrap that round you. Gets a bit cold in here come night, especially when there's mist like tonight. Now, what's your name?'

As he spoke he tinkered with the stove and the good sound of something bubbling became a melodic background to his voice, which was gravel sharp but not unkind.

'Dane.'

'How long you been homeless, Dane?'

'Two weeks.'

'No chance of going back?'

'None.' Dane surprised himself with the vehemence of his reply. The derelict smiled, revealing broken blackened teeth that made him look fearsome.

'Like that, is it? Right, I'm Jonah. Not my real name, you know, something the others been calling me for years, so it's good enough for everyone. Dane. Good solid name, that, bet you come from a good solid family who don't appreciate or understand the needs of a growing boy. Right?'

Dane sat staring at the grimy wall, seeing not the discoloured bricks but his family as he had last seen them... his mother decapitated by the blast of a shotgun, his father with a knife in his neck, spouting blood like a fountain, his older sister screaming her rage and kicking wildly as the

42

intruders tied her and carried her out the door. If he hadn't been under the stairs at the time the men broke in, he would have been dead or carried away too. It was no consolation. The images would not go.

It was my fault. All of it. Shouldn't have happened like that, they were supposed to...

In that moment the sheer desolation of his plight swept over him and he folded up, sobbing helplessly. Jonah reached out a rough hand and pulled Dane close to him. The boy was grateful for the human touch, the first he had known since that terrible time.

'Is it that bad, kid?' Jonah asked in a quiet, serious voice. Dane nodded, sniffing and trying hard to stem the tears. He muttered into the dirty coat: 'Men broke in our house. Shot my Mam, big gun, shotgun, shot her head clean off. One threw a knife, got my Dad in the throat. My sis, Deanna, carried out she was, carried out screaming and yelling and I don't know where they took her. Took the money, took the TV and the stereo and all the nice things we had."

It tumbled out, a mass of words, bringing visions of horror beyond belief for a boy, the amount of blood, the mess his mother's head made on the carpet, the screams of his sister still echoing in his ears.

'And you were hiding, were you? Gone to get something when they came in and they didn't know you was there. Then you ran. Sensible kid you are, Dane, sensible. Down to your bones.' Dane felt an arm go round his shoulders and he snuggled closer to his rescuer. 'And you been on the streets ever since. Too scared to go home. Right?'

Dane nodded. He thought of his home, his aunts and uncles, his grandparents who would by now be involved in arranging funerals while waiting for news of Deanna, if there was any, and of him, for they would think he too had been abducted. He longed for the comfort of the familiar faces, his clothes, books, toys, school friends, all of it left back there, hiding behind the mask of blood and brains that came between him and everything he had left.

'I can't go home,' he whispered.

I can't go home 'cos they know who I am and I know who they are and – oh God, they know, they know, but no one else does, the bullying, the torture, the pain, the need to stop them hurting me all the time. Them, Josh and Ned, had their eyes on Deanna for an age, wanting her, she didn't want them, called them scum and dirtbags and everything and everything they did made it worse for them and worse for me.

Jonah nodded, his wiry beard brushing the top of Dane's head as he did so. 'Course not. Too much blood, too many memories, too scared they might realise you saw them. Course not. You'll be all right with me, little 'un. Now, hungry, are you?'

\*\*\*

After three days of living with Jonah, Dane began to accept his new life with some level of enthusiasm. Without actually saying anything,

44

Jonah showed him where to find cast away food, bought and not eaten most of the time and half empty cans of coke and other drinks in rubbish bins. He rescued a thick sweater from a dump which kept him warm without getting in the way of his sliding the occasional packet of biscuits or candy into a pocket as he passed by the display. Calm, Jonah showed him, calm, no rushing away to draw attention to yourself. Walk as if you had every right to be there. He even managed to ignore the slipperiness underfoot in the alleyway and the strange sensation when he touched the walls, putting it down to damp and decay. It was a good enough explanation without asking questions and not liking the answers.

All was good and Dane was content until he brought home a newspaper for Jonah and saw his face staring out from the front page. Beside his photo was one of Deanna, which brought tears to his eyes. He threw the paper down and stared at Jonah.

'Now I can't go out.'

'Oh yes you can, boy, yes you can. Wait for tonight. 'Tis a full moon, if I reckon it right and we can do something which will let you go out. If you're up for it, of course.'

'Depends on what it is.'

But the boy in Dane was intrigued; even as the more mature person street life was creating thought the words were nonsensical. He was himself, how could he be any different?

'Wait and see and I'll tell you nearer the time. Don't want you worrying yourself for nothing, do we?'

'Suppose not. Suppose I get to stay here until then.'

'Right on. You rest up, tis my turn to go get the food in. I wouldn't mind a beer, either.'

Jonah shambled his way out of the alley, leaving Dane in the darkness with his thoughts. What did Jonah have in mind? How could he be changed? Then the doubts set in; should he give himself up to the police, put the family's mind at rest that at least one of the children had survived? No, that was out of the question. Deanna was no doubt dead by now, she wouldn't be allowed to live; she had seen everything. If he went to the police, his picture would be everywhere and they'd find him. Definitely they would find him. He did not want to die. He had a lot to do.

They made it clear, over and over, those two and the hangers-on they attracted, made it clear they were prepared to kill if they had to. And I believed them. Why not? They thieved and mugged and tortured and never once did the cynical smiles leave their faces. Never once.

He sat still, listening to the road noise: sirens, engines, horns, the crump of metal as car hit car, then the other sounds filtered in, a plane screaming its way into the airport, the rhythmic thump of a helicopter circling the area – traffic reports, I bet, thought Dane – voices, laughter, shouts, cries. It seemed as if the more he lived on the streets the clearer everything became, he had never been so aware of how much noise there was in a city. Or how much there was to fear. Any of those noises could mean danger for him, any of them could mean one of the two had found out where he was and made up his mind to come and get him...

He heard shuffling and tensed, his stomach contracting in sick fear, but Jonah's gravel voice assured him all was well.

'Got us some good food here, boy, got me some good beer, too. Oh, got a Coke for you, a new one. Here, enjoy!'

'I'm glad you're back!' Dane got up hugged his friend in a rare display of emotion. It seemed to take Jonah by surprise, for he sat down and stared at Dane for some time. Then he coughed and put both hands to his head.

'Damn me, boy, been a good many years since someone did that.'

'Sorry...'

'Don't you be sorry none! It were wonderful, that it were.'

They sat in silence for a while, lost in their thoughts, not able to share. Dane had some heavy burdens on his mind; they were not for Jonah, who had enough of his own.

'Right.' Jonah was all briskness and efficiency. 'Get this food in you, tis a bit warm still and good for you right now. Then we can talk.'

Talk. They had talked endlessly for three days and yet Jonah said they were to talk. Dane had stuck to his story and Jonah had respected that, not asking any questions, accepting what Dane told him. They had talked of his past life up to that time, of school, friends, family, Christmasses and birthdays, things he would never have dreamed of sharing with someone but it felt good, reliving those happy times felt so very good, covering up the pain and guilt that was otherwise tearing him apart. Where was Deanna now? Was she still alive and suffering at their hands? What brutal sex had she endured, for it was a given that they would have taken her, it was what they wanted and Dane knew it. It made the guilt even worse. But when all that had been told, all the good times and the bad times, everything but the truth of that day, what else was there to turn over and dissect – unless Jonah had an idea of what had really happened.

'Bit of fun, Daney boy, bit of fun. Let us in, we'll take Deanna away for a little while, you know, wind her up a bit, we won't harm her none, promise. We need to show her we're good guys at heart. She's got the wrong opinion of us, hasn't she? You know what we're like.'

Oh yes, he knew what they were like but with a knife carving a line down his chest, drawing a trickle of blood he knew would be obvious to his mother if she saw it, with Ned standing by tapping a staple gun on the table as if he was longing to use it on flesh, not on the table which was already studded with a thousand staples, what choice did he have?

Now I know how Judas felt. He got himself in a situation and he couldn't get out of it. If I'd've reported these bastards for bullying a year ago, six months ago, I wouldn't be here now, being carved

48

with a knife and threatened with a staple gun and I wouldn't be seriously betraying my sister.

Only it wasn't like that.

Oh but it was, Dane! It was!

Betrayal. You told them when she would be home, you told them the best time to come, you opened the door to them, Dane! Opened the damned door for them, you did!

And hid when they charged in. And threw up when the shotgun went off. And ran when you saw the mess they made when they were done.

Somehow he ate the food, warm and tasty and filling, he noted. The Coke was good too, full of fizz. Everyone before this had gone flat, leaving only the taste behind and without the bubbles, it wasn't the same.

He almost felt like a human being again, not a guilt ridden wreck of a teenager who had somehow gotten on the wrong side of a gang of bullies who had terrified him. With appalling consequences.

What did Jonah have in mind?

The old man seemed to take an age to eat his food. Maybe he had bad teeth, mused Dane, ones that made it hard to eat, maybe it hurt to eat. Whatever, he wished Jonah would hurry so they could get on with the talking. He had the feeling it was big, serious and scary all at the same time. Thinking on that, did he want Jonah to stop eating and start talking?

His stomach said no. His heart said yes. Somewhere in the middle his brain decided it had no feelings one way or the other, provided he stayed safe, which was all that mattered to him.

Outside of the need for revenge, that was.

Revenge. That burning need to take the two men and their hangers'-on and torment them the way they had tormented him. To draw a long open bleeding raw line down their chests, carve their initials in the living skin, watch them writhe under the blade, watch them lose control of themselves when they realised that the victim had become the killer. For he would, he would without a second thought, kill them stone dead. And walk away and be proud of what he had done.

'Been watching your thoughts, boy.' Jonah sucked at the bottle of beer and looked at Dane. 'You show your emotions a bit easy, you know, but then you trusts old Jonah, don't you?'

Dane nodded, but said nothing.

'I saw your face; it went from fear to anger and determination. I think, tell me I'm wrong, boy, if I am, tell me I got it completely wrong but if you found those men who took your family from you, there would be killing, right?'

'Right.' Dane stared back at Jonah. 'What chance...'

'Every chance. One step at a time, boy, one step at a time. We're dealing with the full moon tonight; we gotta get past this bit first and then see where we go. Nearly Halloween, we can do things that night we can't do other nights, but first we have to make ourselves ready.'

The lantern flickered out. Dane felt a sliver of ice go through him. The darkness was all consuming, impenetrable, frightening. A hand touched his shoulder and he stifled a shriek. Jonah

50

grunted with amusement. 'Tis only me, boy, who else did you think would be in here?'

'The lantern...'

'Ran out of fuel, is all. But as it happens, it's good. What we have to say is best said in the dark.'

The silence between them was as thick as the darkness itself. Dane felt he had to say something but couldn't find the words. If Jonah would only speak...

He did but then Dane wished he hadn't.

'So, what really happened, boy? Tis a lot more to that story than you be telling.'

'How ... how did you know?'

'You be too well educated, too – cared for, to be a true runaway. No one after you in the family, no parents beating you up, nothing like that. Am I right? No need to answer, I know I am. So, what happened that day?'

'I...' The words spilled suddenly, the darkness helping to hide his emotions and Jonah's.

'These guys, they were in the last year at school when I started. They picked on me from the start, don't know why, do they need a reason to bully someone? Stole my money, books, clothes; twisted my arm, near enough dislocated my shoulder one time when I tried to fight back. Then they took to following me everywhere. School's been a time of terror; never thought it would end. Some days they wouldn't be there, other days they would. Never knew what and where and why. They followed me home and they saw Deanna. You saw the picture, Jonah, she's beautiful, right?'

Jonah grunted.

'No one listened to me. Said it was all in my head and I should get on with life. Parents, teachers, friends, no one believed me 'cos no one saw them near me, they took good care of that. Then they left and I thought I was free. No. They went right on following me, taking me to their hideout, burning me with cigarettes, cutting me with their knives, because they wanted Deanna and she didn't want them.

'When it got serious, when they were threatening to kill me, I had to do what they wanted, tell them when she would be home. They said it was a joke. I knew it wasn't. I went to the cops that night but they laughed at me and told me to go home. I did. Next day they burst in and shot Mum and Dad...' He faltered, gathered his strength and went on. 'Now I want nothing more than to find them and kill them. Slowly. The slower the better. Starve them to death. Pay them back for years of torment and what they did to my family. I'll pay any price – any price at all – to do that.'

'Mercy save us, that's one hell of a story, boy. You been holding a lot in for a lot of years and it all blew up in the end. Damnation on those cops who laughed at you, I say. Right...'

The figure stirred in the darkness and Dane thought, for a moment, he saw an outline of light around Jonah. Impossible, the blackness was impenetrable. He wasn't afraid and for the first time, he felt as if he was purged of all that the hurt he had suffered all the years.

'I can help you, Dane. I can help you but there's a price.'

'What?'

'You won't be the same again when we're through.'

'Not sure what you mean.'

'Course you don't. I'm not the derelict you think I am, boy, I got powers. I been helping people best I can for a goodly number of years, that I have, with the help of a dark angel. You know what I mean, boy?'

'A demon?'

'Right first time. I wasn't sure about him and you; not till the day you give me that hug. Ain't no one done that in a mountain of years. Rare touched my heart, that did and he spoke with me that night, spoke in my head like he does, asked me to find out your story and he would see what he could do. He's right here alongside me now. He's ready to change you, Dane, change you just a little so you can do what you need to do.'

'I can't change back, is that what you're saying?'

'Right, boy. Right first time. Your choice. You get this one chance and then, who knows? You could go back to what's left of your family.'

A sudden longing swept through Dane, to be held by his loving grandmother for a moment, to see his grandfather's friendly grin and go fishing with him, to see his aunts and uncles, all would be sorrowing over the deaths and thinking he was dead, too.

'How do I go back?'

'One step at a time. Ain't I told you that already? Tonight's the full moon. Tonight you can take that first step, let the dark angel here change you. Then you get your revenge, then you see how you can go home. One step, another step, another step. Tis important, Dane, boy, tis important you know you won't be the same – after.'

'Will anyone else know I am different?'

'Nope. You thought I was just some old drunk, didn't you? You ain't thought any different all the time you've been here, right?'

'And you were changed?'

'Sure enough was. Most drunks get murdered by hoodlums and thrill seekers. Not Jonah.'

'Don't you want to go home?'

Jonah sighed and the sound was every sad thing Dane had ever heard.

'I had a wife, Dane. Right beautiful she was too; most beautiful thing ever walked this earth. Loved her beyond all sense and reason, I did. She was mugged right out there in the street, smashed her lovely face in, he did. I went to drink then and ended up here and the dark angel found me and showed me how to get my revenge. Cornered him, I did, and smashed his face in, but not like he did hers, I did it slowly, bit by bit, gouged out his eyes one at a time, smashed his nose, tore off his ears, one at a time, cut his mouth until it were a huge blood ridden grin, carved initials into his cheeks and forehead. Then I killed him.'

Dane sat, mouth open, visualising the blood, the pain and the shrieking that would have gone with the killing – and knew he wanted it, wanted it so much it was a physical pain.

'And I never went home because all I had to live for was gone. I thought. Then I found out that sometimes, just sometimes, runaways like you came to find me and I could help them and it makes living just about worthwhile.'

For the second time Dane reached across and hugged his friend, ignoring the smelly coat and the unwashed smell. He didn't fare much better himself.

'I'm ready.'

The darkness alongside Jonah changed; a vivid crimson glow outlined a man, one who appeared to be a solid lump of muscle. The face was almost human, the eyes definitely were not. The glow became stronger and the man, the only way Dane could describe him, became clearer. And terrifying. Dane felt every part that was outside his body trying to crawl into his body and hide.

'We need no lanterns.' The voice was not quite right, someone trying to be human but not quite making it. 'I make light. I make you strong. I make you fit to fight. I make you a killing machine. I give you take. You learn to control it. You agree?'

Dane thought for a moment. He was young enough to want the ability to take revenge and old enough to know he would have a hard job controlling it, but it was worth it. Oh yes, it was worth it.

'I agree.'

It was like burning coals heaped on his head and body; he almost cried out but gritted his teeth and waited as the pain swept through him.

'Hold on, boy!' Jonah was doing his best to help and his voice gave Dane the courage to hang on against all the odds, knowing that sooner or later the pain would go. It was what was giving him his new abilities, he knew that. Even as he thought it, the pain began to lessen, to creep from his feet back up his legs, through his body and finally out through his head.

'Strong person.'

'I knew it,' agreed Jonah. 'I don't give you just anyone, do I?'

'You good servant of the Dark Master.'

'And this one will be, too.'

'You are right.'

Even as he watched, the crimson glow faded and the demon, whatever it was, returned to the darkness. Dane was sure he was still there, though, watching, listening, waiting with the patience only demons can truly know. He wondered why he wasn't afraid.

'Dane, there ain't nothin' you can't do now, boy, short of flying across this city by flapping your arms. You can fight anyone and win. You can stand up to any man and know your look will bring him down, make him back off. You can find the tormentors and you can kill them, as fast or as slow as you want. Your choice. You just got a gift few get, use it well.'

Dane stood up and reached for the grimy ceiling of the alleyway. He felt as if he could

56

punch his way through it, but didn't, his friend would lose his home if he did. He turned round and stared at Jonah.

'That – that stuff – I walked on to get in here and walked on to get out, it isn't animal, is it?'

'Nope.'

'That's what I thought. It's them who tried to mug you for your booze, right? Fools.'

Dane felt about twice his age, in thought and in body. He was ready to go out and find those who had taken his sister and his life, ready to wreak total vengeance on them but Jonah put a hand on his arm and held him back.

'This is the first step, boy, like I told you. Now, rest easy and let it build inside you. Slowly and surely, let it build. All right?'

'Makes sense, yes.'

'Reason I say it, boy, is this. Three days' time it's Halloween. You can go out there on the streets, with mask and costume and everything and go do what you wanna do without anyone seeing you. Right? Then, when it's done and you're satisfied, you can take off the costume and go home.'

Home. If anything was a Halloween dream, it was that, going home, even if it was to fewer people than he had been with before. But home...

Three days.

A small amount of time to wait to pay back years of torment and loss. To take his revenge and then go home with blood on his hands and peace in his heart. Could he live with that?

Jonah must have read his thoughts. 'You can live with it, Dane, my boy, you can live with it because you will have found peace, the kind that only comes when there is blood on your hands.'

Three days to his Halloween dream. Yes, he could wait. But once the magical witching date arrived he would go out into the world –

And the world had better watch out.

Nothing would ever be the same again.

# Mortaki
## Dan Allen

The stairs were narrow. Each step took them farther away from the entrance and into the darkness. Loud thumping shook the house and the walls vibrated with a rhythmic pulse. Buck covered his ears and froze, unable to take the next step.

"I don't want to," he said in a quiet voice that had yet to turn hysterical.

Buck's father squeezed in and gently coaxed his son along. Behind them, the stairwell filled with people pushing and crowding, desperate to reach the top.

"Come on, Buck. We have to go."

"I don't want to. I want to go back."

"We can't now. There are too many people behind us. We need to keep going, little bear. We're blocking the way."

Buck took another step; his tiny knees shaking like a trembling rabbit. Ahead, someone screamed and Buck turned back.

"Keep going, buddy."

Buck wrapped his arms around his dad's leg and held on with a firm grip. Jake lifted his son and carried him.

At the top floor of the haunted house, they waded through a knee-deep green fog. Sounds of a swamp ricocheted off the walls and an owl's screech competed with a thumping jungle drumbeat. The orange glow of a fire cut through the

59

mist and a large black kettle boiled over, clearly the source of the fog.

A witch jumped from the shadows and pressed her face close to Buck and Jake. "Well, what do we have here?"

Jake Underwood felt his son's body stiffen as he clung tighter. "It's okay," he whispered.

"What's your name, little boy?" The witch paused, giving Buck a chance to respond and perhaps save himself. Seeing that fear paralyzed his ability to speak, she stomped her foot, demanding an answer.

"Go ahead, tell her your name, son."

The witch reached for the boy, her fingers unnaturally long and her nails curled in a hideous gnarl. The wart, bent nose and crooked hat completed a vision that leapt from the pages of a storybook. Buck buried his face in his father's shoulder and locked his arms around his neck.

"I'm going to throw you in my stew." The witch cackled and let them pass, content to torment the next child in line.

"I told you I didn't want to come. I told you." Buck's bottom lip quivered as small pools gathered below his eyes.

Funnelled through a hanging gauntlet of severed legs, Jake hurried toward a crack of sunlight marking the exit. Car headlights flashed on and raced toward them, a horn blared and Jake held his breath as he instinctively jumped back. Buck lost his grip and his fingers slipped from his father's hand. The boy slumped to the floor where he sat, flopped on one side like a rag doll.

Most of the visitors to the haunted house remarked that the firefighters outdid themselves with the headlight gag. The annual attraction received rave reviews from everyone, with one exception... Solemn and defeated, Buck's life would never be the same.

***

The child sat in the backseat and refused to speak during the ride home. Later that evening, Jake entered his room to tuck him in.

"Want to give your dad a hug goodnight?"

"I do. But I don't," said Buck, and he pulled the covers over his head.

Night crept towards dawn. Jake awoke to sobbing sounds coming from his son's bedroom.

"I told you not to take him," Sandra said, clearly displeased. "I knew he wasn't old enough to handle a haunted house."

"Alright, already."

"No, it's not alright. Do you know he told me a witch wanted to throw him in the stew? He had tears in his eyes, Jake. Not smiles. Tears."

"C'mon, Sandy. He loves Halloween. Spooky stuff is part of the festivities. He's old enough to handle it."

"Just like he was old enough to watch *Die Hard* because you insisted it was a Christmas movie?"

Jake honestly forgot about the violence and language when he suggested the film, but he knew better than to make excuses. Whenever Sandra was upset, he had learned to smile, nod and keep his mouth shut.

Jake found the boy sitting on the floor beside the bed; his hiccup-like sobs punctuated awkward sniffles.

"What's wrong, little bear?"

"The Munchers are coming." Buck stared at the wall. His pupils remained undilated when Jake waved a hand in his face.

"Did you have a bad dream, buddy? You know there are no Munchers, right?"

"There *are* Munchers, Dad. Mortaki told me all about them."

\*\*\*

A two-foot wide ribbon of morning sun cut through the kitchen and brightened the room. The cat positioned herself perfectly to allow both her head and tail to fit inside the yellow strip of light.

"Honeycombs?"

"Yes, please," replied Buck. The trauma of the previous day appeared to be over.

"Trick-or-Treat is this weekend. Have you decided what you want to be? I could paint your face and make you a vampire."

"Dad, are vampires real?

"No, buddy. They're make-believe."

"Do you think maybe *some* of them are real?"

"Nope. They're only pretend."

"I don't like vampires. Too scary. I want to be something happy."

"Happy, eh? How about I put a big yellow ball over your head and paint a smiley face on it." Jake grabbed the boy under his armpit and squeezed his giggle spot. Buck squirmed away, laughing.

"No, Dad. I want to be a good guy, a superhero!"

"A superhero? We can do that. Which one?"

"The movie guy. I want to be the Black Panther."

Jake nodded. "T'Challa, the king of Wakanda. Sounds like a good choice,"

\*\*\*

That evening, Sandra Underwood stood in the hallway with a finger over her lips. She squinted with her head slightly cocked. "Jake, come here. Quick."

"What is it?"

"Shhh. Quiet."

Jake tiptoed across the cold hardwood floor, chilled by the late October weather. He heard talking and shook his head, certain he could make out two voices.

"No, Mortaki, No... I don't want to. But what about the Munchers? Yes... Yes... Okay... Do you promise?"

Sandra nudged the bedroom door open to find Buck standing in the corner, bare-chested and wearing only his Spiderman pyjama bottoms. He faced the wall with his hands behind his back. His eyes were closed and his head tilted at an awkward angle towards the ceiling. Buck's mouth stayed open and created the perfect illusion of a sleepwalker.

"No, Mortaki!" he screamed, arms flying and little clenched fists swatting at the air.

Jake flinched at the sudden outburst, his knee smashing against the half-opened door. The boy turned, arms falling to his sides. His eyes opened and he looked at his father.

"I'm late for school," Buck said. He climbed into his bed and snuggled under the covers. His soft breathing and the gentle rise and fall of the sheets confirmed he was asleep.

"What the hell was that about?" Jake looked at Sandra for an answer.

"You know what that's about, mister. That's about you forcing a frightened child into a scary haunted house."

"I didn't exactly make him."

"Oh, please. You dragged Buck in there and carried him back out."

\*\*\*

Sandra laid overlapping sheets of newspaper on the kitchen floor while Jake washed dirt off a basketball-sized pumpkin.

"Buck, bring your drawings; it's time to cut this puppy open."

The boy presented a crayon sketch of a classic pumpkin face – triangle eyes and nose, jagged teeth. Jake handed his son a cheap steak knife.

"Carve away."

64

"Oh, no, you don't," Sandra said, taking away the knife and gritting at Jake. "You carve, Buck directs."

Jake worked his magic and created a perfect Halloween jack-o'-lantern. He went off the menu with the eyes, curving them up in the corners, more cat-like than triangular and the overabundant teeth ended up resembling pointed fangs.

"What do you think, Buck ol' boy? Is that scary or what?"

"I like it, Dad. It looks just like my drawing."

"What say you clean up all the pumpkin guts and I'll get us a candle."

"Ew, pumpkin guts! Gross, Dad."

Jake returned a few minutes later and his mouth fell open. He held the doorframe for support, inhaled deeply and let out a sigh as Buck, grasping the knife in a firm overhand grip, slashed away at the pumpkin. He stabbed and repeatedly hacked at what remained of the face.

"Stop!" Sandra pushed into the kitchen and grabbed Buck's arm. "Why, Buck? Why did you do this?" She snatched the knife away and tossed it in the sink.

"He said the Munchers wouldn't like it. He said it was too scary."

Sandra felt her son's head, checking for a fever. "Is this enough festive fun for you, Jake?"

Jake ignored her question. "Who, Buck? Who told you this?"

"Mortaki. Jeez, Dad."

"Buck, you destroyed all our work. Now we won't have a jack-o'-lantern for Halloween."

The boy shrugged, jumped up and scurried away, leaving the shredded pieces of a masterpiece for Jake to clean up.

"Dad," Buck called from another room, "what's a turnip?"

"It's a vegetable, son," Jake mumbled. His mind was not on the question.

"They're no good either," Buck said.

\*\*\*

Buck shifted from one foot to the other and checked the street for the tenth time. He moved around with the anxious fidgeting of a little boy who needs to pee.

"Come on, Dad. Let's go. I see kids out already."

Buck, dressed like a black cat, went as a superhero as planned. Jake thought he looked more like Batman with claws but wasn't going to spoil the kid's fun.

An impossibly large harvest moon illuminated the annual game of dress-up and blackmail. They hit the streets while a smidgen of pale blue sky clung to the western horizon. Buck was determined to accumulate the world's most enormous pile of candy. Jake zipped up his jacket and kept his hands in his pockets. He should have selected something warmer.

The first hour passed, and dusk surrendered to evening.

"Your bag getting too heavy?" Jake asked.

66

"No way. Not even close. I'm not giving in until we visit the big houses up the hill."

Oak Street twisted and turned as it rose to the crest, an unforgiving climb but well worth the effort. The estate homes ranking the ascent offered far better candy than the townhouses below. The barren trees, their leaves having fallen off weeks earlier, looked dead. Jake could see into backyards usually camouflaged with foliage and envied the multi-tier decks and in-ground pools.

An unusual gust of cold air swept through the street. Buck stopped suddenly, frozen in the centre of the sidewalk. Tumbling leaves spun around his feet and switched directions at will.

"I'm big enough," Buck said. "I can do it, Mortaki. I promise."

"Who's Mortaki, your imaginary friend?" Jake was concerned, but the boy ran toward a darkened house. The driveway held no cars and the property bore no decorations. Buck reached the door within seconds, where a little clown, holding a semi-deflated balloon, waited patiently for someone to answer.

"Nobody home there, Buck. Go to the Wilsons. It's the next one over." Jake said.

A miniature Spider-Man and an even smaller Ninja followed Buck to the Wilson driveway. In minimal costumes and without masks, a group of teenagers busily gorged themselves on treats from their booty. They stepped aside to allow the little ones a clear path to the door, where a scarecrow sat propped up in a lawn chair. Weathered straw hung from his boot tops, the waist of his denim jeans and the sleeves of his red lumber jacket. Jake felt suspicious about the scarecrow and moved closer. The teenagers, aware of what was about to happen, shuffled positions for a better view. Hidden speakers began to play an off-key version of the tension-inducing jack-in-a-box song about a monkey chasing a weasel. The eerie music further unnerved Jake.

Mrs. Wilson answered the door. She took one look at Buck and dropped the candy bowl.

"You're not supposed to be here," she said in a deep, angry voice, much unlike her own.

"Trick or treat," said Spider-Man.

"Oh, my. I don't know what came over me," Mrs Wilson said in her usual, pleasant voice while bending over to retrieve a dozen tiny bags of chips. "Now, who do we have here?"

The kids added to their haul and said thanks. Jake flinched at the movement of a gloved hand and, still too distant to warn the children, watched as the scarecrow abruptly stood.

"Happy Halloween, you little rascals!" Mr. Wilson said, and he removed his scarecrow hat.

The Ninja cried, but Buck held it together and remained composed. "Gee wiz, Mr. Wilson. You really scared us good."

"You kids have fun tonight. And be safe."

\*\*\*

ake and Buck headed up the hill toward the next house and Jake noticed a boy approaching. He was the same size as Buck, but his face looked much older. He wore a burlap bag like a dress. His eyes were dark and sunken. Long dirty hair flowed down the sides of his face and over his shoulders.

Creepy costume, Jake thought.

The boy drew closer and Jake saw the dirty bare feet, stained finger, and unclipped nails.

"Hey, it's too chilly to be walking around with bare feet. You're gonna catch a cold," Jake said.

The boy stopped a few feet in front of them. A small gust ruffled his hair. Swirling leaves and the smell of rotting apples followed. He carried no candy sack but instead held a cloth doll by the arm, letting the rest of it drag on the ground.

"You live around here?" Jake asked.

Although he felt the urgent tug on his pant leg, Jake ignored little Buck and stayed focused on the urchin-like stranger. The urchin said nothing but slowly opened his black, toothless mouth and smiled. He raised a hand with four equally long fingers and no thumb, then pointed over Jake's head and down the hill.

A black curtain crept out of the shrinking horizon and slowly began to absorb everything in its path. Sidewalks and houses, lawns and driveways, all flickered like a heat mirage and were swallowed up. The curtain was not exactly a black hole but more like an all-consuming entity that left nothing behind but an imageless void. Jake heard the distant sucking sound, slurping and crunching. Underground pipes moaned and twisted as they ripped from the ground and electrical wires sparked for a brief second before vanishing into the advancing emptiness. A whiff of ozone hung in the air before it, too, was consumed and sanitized into nothing.

Jake stood frozen in place, mouth hanging open as he watched the void creep closer. He wanted to run but couldn't decide where to go. Buck remained calm as if watching the city bus approach instead of the end of the world. He tugged harder on his father's pant leg and Jake finally looked down at his son.

"Munchers," Buck said, with the seriousness of someone much older. He squeezed his father's hand. "Come on, Dad."

The urchin blocked their path, then began taking exaggerated steps backwards, easily outpacing Jake and his son. He smiled and his lips curved over his gums, creating the illusion of an exceptionally long chin. He slowed so the father and son could close the distance and, as soon as they were within an arm's reach, the urchin spat on young Buck.

"Hey, kid. What the hell are you doing?" Jake lunged for the guttersnipe, but the urchin fled, darting up the hill and disappeared into the night. His laughter trailed behind, forced and exaggerated, bouncing from one side of the street to the other until it too faded away with one last whisper and an echo.

The streetlights blinked dim, then bright and finally settling on fading out completely. The lights in the homes lining the hill shut off in a rolling sequence. A dark purple glow covered the neighbourhood in a silent dome. No leaves rustled on the sidewalk and the air remained still.

Jake felt pale and stumbled near collapse. The blood drained from his face and his shirt stuck to his back. A cold breeze rippled over his arm hair and he could hear his pulse.

*Not now, damn it. Keep it together, keep it together.* He talked himself out of the panic attack and focused on his son.

"You okay, Buck?" Jake saw his own breath. A damp chill stung his cheek.

"We don't have much time, Dad."

The silence was uncanny. No traffic. No excited cries of children trick or treating. It all disappeared with the house lights. Only the orange glow from candles in carefully carved pumpkins escaped the blackout. They made an eerie contrast to the purple air.

"Where did everybody go?" Jake, stunned and confused, dragged his feet and looked heavenward. The oversized moon no longer brightened the sky and even the stars refused to show themselves.

Buck tugged on his dad's wrist and tried to keep him moving along. Crunching sounds, stomping like an industrial press, chattered the silence and startled Jake back into action.

They moved through the purple fog, following the light escaping from pumpkins standing sentry on each doorstep. Their carved faces, no longer smiling, now appeared sinister and snarling. As Buck and his dad passed each driveway, the flame inside the jack-o'-lantern bent itself between crooked teeth and stretched downhill, creating a long thread of fire. The void sucked it in, stealing the heat and light. The extinguished pumpkin rolled itself to the curb in preparation for the imminent black curtain.

"Pick up your feet, Buck. We need to go faster," Jake said, fully aware of the danger bearing down on them.

A beacon glowed from the crest of the hill. A lone flame waved from a candle propped in the grand window of the Millar mansion. The house pre-dated the subdivision by a century, and its position above the valley commanded a powerful view.

"This way, Dad. Run!"

Cement crumbled and broke apart, releasing billowing clouds of toxic dust that nipped at their heels. The Millar's driveway pitched and rolled like an ocean wave. Jake hoisted his boy up with one arm. He struggled to keep his balance and ascended the front steps with a drunken stagger. Not an eyelash of light escaped from the slightly open double French doors. Jake dove headfirst into the unknown. Buck landed atop him as they slid over the marble floor.

Once across the threshold, the foyer sparkled to life under the umbrella of a fabulous chandelier. At the bottom of the grand staircase stood an old man dressed in a tailed tuxedo with a maroon ascot in place of a tie. His white hair cascaded over his shoulders and his long arms bent back awkwardly at the elbows. He was tall and hovered over Buck and his dad. An image of a praying mantis flashed through Jake's mind.

"I am Mortaki, master of this humble abode. You are Jake Underwood, I presume. Buck, I have met. I must say, governor, you spared no time getting here. Cut it mighty damn close if you ask me."

Mortaki closed the thick oak doors and turned the centre deadbolt. The world eater paused its advance and the blackness waited at the edge of the property line. As if angered by the delay, storm clouds formed and circled the mansion. Gale-force winds whistled as they revved up and ripped at the outer walls. The front picture window rattled in its old wooden frame and a small crack skated from a corner, sliced across the glass and threatened to spill out a waterfall of shards. The lonely candle flame, still burning, flickered and swayed in a dance all its own.

"What have you done, Jake? Look at the destruction you have caused." Mortaki offered Jake a hand and pulled him from the floor.

Mortaki's grip was firm for an old man and Jake felt uncomfortable in his presence. Despite the sanctuary of his home, he disliked the lanky elder and was suspicious, maybe even jealous, of Buck's apparent infatuation with him.

Jake studied his son and watched as the boy removed his panther costume and fold it neatly on a wingback chair.

"Why'd you take off your costume, Buck?"

"It's not time for trick or treats, Dad. Isn't that right, Mortaki?"

In the far corner, a familiar rag doll sat slumped headfirst against the baseboard. Buck scurried over and retrieved it. A panel slid open and a four-fingered hand grabbed the boy's collar and pulled him behind the wall.

Jake charged to the spot and slapped at the panelling, desperate to locate the secret door. Finding nothing, he pounded on the wood and screamed.

"Mortaki! Where's my son?" Veins in Jake's neck bulged as he spat out the words. He turned to face the white-haired man, but Mortaki was gone.

"You torment your children with stories of monsters." Mortaki's voice came from above and echoed in the empty room.

Jake stood alone, staring at the ceiling and heard a second voice.

"I'm here, Dad. Over here."

Jake ran into the adjoining room, a study with a double-wide fireplace. The hearth was cold and unused.

"You entertain them with programs depicting violence and slaughter." Mortaki's voice again came from above, but it sounded even farther away than the ceiling.

"Buck, can you hear me?" Jake called.

"You dress them up and take them to dark places of make-believe, exposing them to cult-like activities."

"I'm here, Dad. Help me!"

"Activities that worship the dead and celebrate evil."

Jake watched the contours of the ceiling and followed them into a library, the walls lined with leather-bound books and the shelf edges lined with dust.

"How much can their little minds sustain, Mr Underwood? How much, I ask you?"

"Here, Dad. This way." Buck's voice called from farther away and Jake backtracked to a sitting room beyond the front hall.

"You exposed your boy to powerful entities, dark and evil forces. Humans are so reckless with their children."

"It's only Halloween," whispered Jake.

"Your son prayed to them. He begged them to take it away, the costumes, the haunted houses, the wicked jack-o'-lanterns, all of it, Mr. Underwood, all of Halloween. The people, the buildings, everything."

Mortaki's voice sounded closer now and Jake followed it back to the grand foyer. He found the conjurer standing exactly where he saw him last. The mantis-like man approached with an awkward jerk as if his legs slightly preceded his body. The rest of him struggled to catch up before his legs moved again. He slinked from the corner and stood by the bannister, his old, wrinkled eyes now twinkling and boring directly into Jake.

"Give me my son," Jake demanded.

Mortaki raised a hand and gestured to the front yard.

"This is his wish, his world, but you created it, Underwood. You set it in motion and enabled it to happen."

"I'm sure you had a part to play, you bastard."

Mortaki shrugged and lowered his head to hide a smile.

"There must be something I can do," Jake spoke aloud and to himself, but his words carried.

"You can do nothing. Only your son has the power to send them away. But he must do it alone, without you."

"Fair enough," said Jake, not knowing for sure what he intended to do and not willing to promise anything to the mantis.

The gale picked up to hurricane force and the windows imploded, spraying needles of glass into Victorian-era wallpaper. The candle, its flame extinguished, fell to the floor, sliced in half. The storm rumbled louder than anything Jake had experienced and the sound left him concussed. Lightning flashed within the house, directly above the grand staircase. Buck materialized on the steps and tumbled the rest of the way down. He came to a rest at his father's feet, none the worse for wear.

"Thanks for finding me, Dad."

Jake smiled and nodded. *I didn't find you, not really,* he thought.

Buck marched towards the exit, fully confident in what he was about to do. The French doors split and opened themselves. Freezing air blasted into the room and the force pinned Jake to the wall. He could only watch as his little boy fought his way down the driveway. The wind pulled at the child's clothes and squeezed the skin flat on his cheeks.

Jake's heart ripped open, and he made a move to chase after his son. "Come back, Buck!" he yelled, but the words faded in the storm.

Fingers pinched Jake's shoulder, the nails pressing through his jacket and holding him firm. A shadow loomed above him and Jake felt warm breath upon his neck.

"He must go alone, governor!" Mortaki shouted in his ear loud enough to be heard over the gale.

Buck stood in front of the endless void, hands on his hips. Unintimidated, he pointed to the left and then the right. Jake could see Buck's lips moving, but the wind obscured any meaning. The boy threw his hands in the air as if he were releasing invisible doves. A chill crept around Jake's collar and spread across his back. He shivered with fear. Dread weighed him down, anchoring him in place. Buck turned his head towards his father and shrugged.

"No, Jake. Don't do it!"

The boy either couldn't hear or chose not to. Eyes closed, he raised his arm and punctured the wall with a single finger. An explosion of light ripped apart the dark fabric of the curtain, shredding it into specs of stardust, scattering it like a fourth of July flare. Violent winds continued to circle and they rose above the mansion, twisting themselves into a tight funnel before vanishing into the atmosphere. For a second, there was silence. Someone screamed—a silly, happy squeal.

A full moon illuminated a street filled with children dressed in colourful costumes. Pirates, witches and zombies crisscrossed the road to carry out their candy-collecting chores. A stream of leaves chased one another over the pavement and swirled around Jake's legs. He smiled and released a lung full of stale air. All was right in the world.

Buck came running to him and he went down on a knee to embrace his son. Jake's eyes watered and threatened to leak; his emotions overflowed with pride and relief.

Buck bypassed his dad, heading instead toward the open French doors.

"What are you doing? Don't go back in there, Buck. Come back!"

"I have to go, Dad. I forgot my costume."

The doors snapped shut behind the boy. Jake remained unmoving and held his head. He mumbled a mantra, *came back, came back,* and prayed for his son's return. Moments later, the doors opened and Jake's happy little black panther appeared, dressed and ready to resume the fun.

Buck bounced around and shifted from foot to foot. He tugged on Jake's pant leg and pointed to a whimsical group of princesses decked out in flowing pastel-coloured dresses with matching ribbons in their hair.

Jake looked back at the Millar estate, silhouetted by the yellow glow of the impossibly large harvest moon and glimpsed something in an upstairs window. He thought maybe the curtain moved and a hand slapped the glass, or perhaps it only waved.

"Did you see that?" he asked Buck, but the boy shook his head.

Beneath the superhero costume, sunken eyes glowed like embers and sharp claws from a thumbless hand poked through the black jungle cat gloves.

"Trick or treat," whispered the urchin.

78

# Darkness Follows
## Carie Juettner

She gathers her robe around her body and pours a whiskey. Her gray hair is long and falls across her shoulders like a cat curled up for a nap. All the lights are off. One tall candle burns in a taper on the coffee table. She sips and speaks.

"Fifty-eight years ago tonight. Fifty-eight years without him."

It's Halloween.

"Don't use that foul word with me. You think I don't know? You think I don't wear the calendar as a collar around my neck, every day leading up to this one a weight in the chain I drag around? Don't say that word to me."

A squeal echoes down the chimney with the wind and she gulps her drink, reaches for the bottle.

No pumpkins and popcorn balls then? No treats?

"No treats. Always tricks."

Tricks… and whiskey. A treat for you.

"Not a treat. This drink is for John. I take no pleasure in it."

And where is John, your little brother? How old is he now?

"Nine. Always nine."

A tap sounds from the front of the house. Then more taps. Then a thumping, a pounding.

There is someone at your door, friend.

She shakes her head and her catlike hair stretches, then curls up again. "That's just John."

So he lives still? He's out there?

Another pour. Another shake. "I've buried John. Over and over I've buried him. John has enough graves to fill a cemetery. But every year he comes knocking."

She fills her glass until the whiskey pools around the rim, hovers briefly, then spills over. The knocking continues. She does not answer.

\*\*\*

"My bag is heavier," the boy says.

"No way. Feel this." His sister swings her pillowcase of candy and hits him in the butt with it. The boy laughs. There is nothing better than Halloween. Nothing sweeter than being out alone at night with the smell of jack-o-lanterns filling your nose and ten pounds of candy weighing down your arm. Well, not alone. He's with his big sister. But no parents. No adults. It's a different world when the adults disappear. A better one.

"Where to next?" They stop at a corner. The boy looks left and right, but he only pretends to contemplate the decision. It doesn't matter what he thinks. He'll follow wherever she leads.

He looks up at her. She's staring at something behind him, her mouth twisted up into a pucker, her bottom lip between her teeth. "What is it?" he asks, whirling around. A Snickers goes spinning out of his bag.

"Nothing. Let's go."

"What were you looking at?"

"Nothing. Just a shadow or something. Come on, let's go to Stillwood. See who's got candy there."

The boy peers into the darkness, wondering how his sister could have seen a shadow when everything is the color of night. More and more houses have extinguished their porch lights, and there is no moon. "Are you trying to scare me?" He fakes a laugh.

"Like I'd even have to try," she says and sprints across the street toward Stillwood.

The boy yells, "Wait for me!" and follows.

\*\*\*

The old woman paces the room, her robe flapping dangerously close to the flickering candle flame. "He shouldn't't've run off like that! He shouldn't't've run into the darkness without me!" Her arm flaps outward, pointing at nothing, sloshing her drink onto the threadbare carpet.

You told him to go. It was you who sent him into the darkness.

She whirls around, eyes closed, forehead pinched. "No, I—"

Yes.

"Yes. But not—I only sent him away to keep him safe, to rescue him. I didn't know—"

Didn't you?

She shakes her head and covers her face with her wrinkled arms. "I didn't know."

How long did you search?

81

"Years. Every hour, every day, every week. Every little boy in jeans and a skeleton t-shirt. Every rustle in every bush."

But eventually you stopped. Eventually you knew.

She drops her arms and collapses into a chair. She wraps her fingers around the tumbler of whiskey. Her hand shakes.

Maybe, deep down, you wanted to lose him.

She brings her glass slowly, deliberately, to her lips.

"Maybe I did."

\*\*\*

More lights wink out as they head to Stillwood. One by one, kids in polyester capes and hooded masks trudge up porch steps and disappear behind doors. The noise fades along with the light until the voices of the boy and his sister are the only ones echoing off fences and sinking into drainage ditches. They jab at each other with their plastic swords and die elaborate deaths on the cracked sidewalks and are mourned by no one but the stars.

Once, the boy's sister glances behind them and frowns. "Huh," she says. But that is all. She keeps walking. He tags along.

At Stillwood, they pause. To the left, there are still a few houses with lit porches. "Jackpot," his sister says. She turns to the boy, a look of mischief on her face and says, "Why don't we—" She stops, her gaze drifting over his shoulder to something behind him.

"What is it?" the boy asks.

"Nothing."

But he turns and it's not nothing. A black shadow, darker than the night around it, and deep, like a hole you could fall into, slouches toward them a block away. A quick sweep of the street reveals they are the last trick-or-treaters. Everyone else is gone. Home. Safe. They are out, at night, alone, on Halloween, and something vaguely shaped like a man is making a steady, hungry beeline for them.

The boy cannot tear his eyes away. With each blink, the thing gets closer, so he tries not to blink, holds his eyelids open until his eyes water and tears spill down his cheeks. He wipes them away, worried his sister will see, and when he looks again the thing has gained two houses on him.

"What is it?" his voice comes as if from a well and takes a long time to reach his own ears.

His sister shakes her head. "Come on." She takes him by the elbow, something his mother used to do, and escorts him across the street and down Stillwood, to the left, toward the last lit houses.

\*\*\*

"I used to call him Leech. Always hangin' on. After our mother was gone, it was like he expected me to coddle him the way she did. Tie his shoes, kiss his scrapes, tuck him in."

He was only five.

"And I was only ten. Didn't I deserve the rest of my childhood? Didn't I deserve a little space?"

So you hid from him.

"Lot of good it did me. That boy could find the needle in the haystack *and* the thread. Never could shake him. Finally quit trying."

There is silence. Deep silence. Vacant silence. She realizes the knocking has stopped. "Quit trying," she repeats.

Until Halloween.

"I told you not to say that word."

Until that night. The night you finally lost him.

"It wasn't... we weren't alone that night. Something else was there. I thought—I thought if we split up—"

You thought about how you were older, stronger. You thought about how your legs were longer, how you could run faster.

"No. No. Well, yes. I did. I thought it would come for me. I thought I could get away."

And you did get away, didn't you?

She hovers in the middle of the room, hand to forehead, eyes closed, swaying slightly.

How long? How long until you knew it hadn't picked you?

She clutches both hands to her face, then opens her eyes, grabs her glass from the coffee table, brings it to her mouth, gulps air.

Your glass is empty, friend.

The knocking begins again. Louder.

\*\*\*

The shadow is gaining on them. No matter how fast they run, how much they zigzag, how many yards

84

they cut through or fences they jump, the darkness behind them gains. Too scared to think of dropping their heavy bags, they leave a trail of candy behind them—like Hansel and Gretel with breadcrumbs made of sweets and something worse than a witch on their tail.

The boy risks another glance back. The shadow is more defined now. It has a profile and legs and a wide-brimmed hat and a curtain of flowing darkness that flutters behind it like a cape. He becomes mesmerized searching for eyes in the blackness and his sister pulls him, her breath a rough scrape against his ear as she growls, "Hurry."

But hurry where? Stillwood is a dead-end street of dark porches and extinguished jack-o-lanterns, the smell of singed pumpkin drifting on the wind. Weren't there lights on just a moment ago? Didn't they see candles burning when they turned? Every last light has winked out now. Curtains are drawn, doors shut, gauzy ghosts snagged on tree branches or laying facedown in driveways, forgotten. There is nothing, no one. Only his tennis shoes on the sidewalk and his sister's ragged breath and her tight grip on his elbow.

And then that too is gone.

The boy's arm is free. Cold air brings goosebumps to the hot skin where her fingers used to be. He stops running, looks around. She's still there, beside him, but her eyes are far away.

"We have to split up," she says. "It can't chase us both."

"But—"

"It will pick me."

"But—"

"It'll be okay. I know a trick."

"What trick? What—"

"Trust me."

The feel of fingers on his arm fades. The goosebumps spread to the rest of his body. He has no answer to this. Of course he trusts her. He always has. The boy nods, but his sister is not looking at him. Her gaze is behind them. He cannot make himself turn to look at what she sees.

"It's going to chase me. Hide until it's gone. Then go home. I'll see you there."

The boy nods again, and this time she pulls her eyes away from the darkness and looks at him. "I'll see you at home," she says again. "Go."

Then she's gone.

And the boy is alone.

Only he's not alone. He has only run a few yards when he feels a pull behind him, an urge to turn and look, and when he does, he sees the shadow, following. It grows closer with every step he takes.

*** 

She drops the empty glass onto the sofa and covers her ears.

Why not let him in?

"Because he's not there! He's never there!" She's shouting, but neither her shouts nor her pressing hands can block out the pounding, which seems to reverberate off the floors and the walls and her bones. "He's not there. I looked everywhere!"

If you'd looked everywhere, you would have found him.

She screams.

*** 

The boy is panting now. It is Halloween. It is dark. He is alone. But not alone enough. He runs, whimpering with each footfall. Willing a light to come on in one of the dark houses. Praying for a friendly face to pull back a curtain and beckon him in.

There is a sound behind him now. Or rather a lack of sound. A silence follows. Behind him there is no breeze. No leaf scuttles. No tree branch creaks. No footsteps scrape behind his on the sidewalk. But the soundless shape rushes on, sucking in night and noise and exhaling a cold fear that is now close enough to nip at the back of the boy's neck.

He's at the last house on the street and the thing is only one driveway behind him. This address is as dark and uninviting as the rest. More so for there is no evidence of the holiday here. No witches dangle from tree limbs. No pumpkins line the porch steps. No orange and black streamers adorn the chain-link fence. Here the cobwebs are real.

What choice does he have? The silence grows closer.

The boy opens the gate, slips past weeds and briar that grab at his legs and hurries up the cracked paving stones to the deep, wrap-around porch. The wooden steps are covered in a layer of dusty dirt. No trick-or-treaters have disturbed this door tonight. He hesitates and looks behind him.

The street is gone. Just beyond the fence, a blackness rises, absorbing the view, cutting off all behind it. One shadowy arm rests on the gate.

The boy swallows and hurries up the steps, his feet raking gouges in the grime. He gets to the heavy wooden door and throws his knuckles against it—once, twice, three times, four, again, and again, and again, knocking so steadily that the sound blocks out any other noise—or absence of it—behind him.

No one comes. He knocks and he knocks and he knocks. But no one comes.

\*\*\*

Her scream dissolves into a hoarse shriek. She rushes toward the door—arms stretched out, gray hair tangling. She throws herself against the wood, fingers splayed, nails piercing the paint.

"It's. Just. A. Damn. Trick-or-treater." The words slip out between her clenched teeth, syncopated between the rhythm of the knocking.

It's John. You already said so. Every Halloween he comes knocking.

She pounds the wood with her fists, growls, "No!" But she is already stepping back, already making room for the door to open.

Let him in, friend. Let him in once and for all.

She reaches for the lock. She turns it. She grips the cold metal knob in her hand and twists.

\*\*\*

The boy stops. He rests his sore knuckles against the splintered wood, against the safety that will not let him in, and looks behind him. The darkness has swallowed the porch steps. It looms in front of him, immense, eyeless, and as silent as the tomb.

He turns back around and pounds the door with both hands, hammering and sobbing until he feels a cold emptiness lay its fingers upon his hair.

He screams.

\*\*\*

The heavy door swings inward.

One crisp fall leaf skitters across the threshold and onto the toe of the old woman's slipper. The porch is silent, empty, save for a pillowcase on the doormat, overflowing with miniature candy bars and bubble gum.

She shuffles across the boards, not noticing when her foot bumps a plastic sword and sends it sliding into the bushes. The clock in the dining room strikes twelve, as a draft of stale air wafts out of the house, lifting the tail of her gray hair as it passes.

See you next year, Sis.

She sinks onto the top porch step, waiting for the night to end, knowing that in the morning, she'll have to bury him again.

# Collecting Treats
## Daniel L. Naden

The number of trick-or-treaters was finally starting to dwindle and amid his festively decorated porch and lawn, George Marsh had nearly finished his window shopping. He was ready to go do the real thing. He'd been parked in a lawn chair from the time when the last of the twilight drained from the October sky drawing out the first children, out in search of candy, until now when the night had descended completely, the chilly wind was whispering secrets amid the bare branches and fallen leaves.

All evening, George handed out treats as children paraded enticingly by him and he commented about their costumes: "There's a scary ghost!" or "Mercy! How frightening!" or "Who are you supposed to be, Princess?"

All evening long, he watched as cautious parents followed along in cars in the street or along the sidewalk, keeping an eye on their children - keeping them safe. Of course, not all the children were accompanied by their parents. Not nearly all. George didn't always go shopping on Halloween, but some of his best shopping trips had come on the one night when kids and chaos ruled the neighborhoods after dark. He'd been planning for this night for months.

So George Marsh teased and laughed with the trick-or-treaters who visited him and while he did, he shopped, he browsed, making note of the children who were alone or in small groups. Eventually, the number of children and parents would thin out and the number of neighbors still giving out treats would dwindle, leaving just a few groups scattered sparsely around the neighborhood. Soon, he would turn off his front porch light, slip out the back, and go on his own trick-or-treating adventure.

In the deepest dark of the October night, he would find what he was looking for: that girl straggling alone from her group, a boy running ahead of his parents, or some carefree group of two or three kids, heading home, comfortable of their own sense of safety in numbers.

But the children were not safe. Not from George Marsh.

When he was out shopping, collecting children, George was quiet and deceptively strong for his short, thin frame. He had a classic runner's build-- lean, wiry--and backed it up with an unflinching will to act. He could slide between the shadows like a knife through fog, but when the time came, he closed quickly.

He had only to get near enough for a quick shot from a chloroform-soaked rag, clasped over the nose and mouth and the child would collapse into his arms to be carried through the shadows back to his house. Once there, George would celebrate his own particularly brutal form of Halloween for as long as the child lasted. Sometimes the children died quickly. Sometimes George's Halloween celebration continued for several days.

***

The night belonged to George. Always, he had felt more at home in the dark than he did anywhere else--always he found an affinity for moving around on foot unnoticed, found a freedom in the anonymity the shadows brought him.

On this night, two nights before Halloween, George slipped out for his last scouting trip. He'd been out every night for the past two weeks: searching for hiding spots, planning walking paths and escape routes, timing patrol patterns for the local police and the various night owls and nosy neighbors who might be out and about. George was a cautious man. You didn't shop, or buy, for as long as he had without being careful. Without preparing exhaustively to reduce as much as possible the risks involved in doing the kinds of things he did on his shopping trips, he was just another scumbag predator, on the hunt for cheap opportunities that would invariably end in jail, or worse. George was better. He was dedicated. His preparation made him, not only successful, but a veritable ghost.

George spent the previous week familiarizing himself with the nearby neighborhoods, matching up real streets and alleys and houses with the ones he'd seen from online maps. These past few days, George watched people, mapping out which homes had lights, or fences, or outside dogs. It was boring, painstaking work that he undertook with a detached air: passionless and devoid of emotion. He had always been able to separate the anticipation of the outcome of his shopping trip from the work of preparing for it. He pushed back the pulse of excitement, banked it against the time when he could let it run free.

*** 

By necessity, his Halloween activities forced him to move every couple of years. His time in this town, this house, was almost done. George had planned on slipping over to the far side of town to do his shopping this afternoon, but he'd heard on his police scanner of an increased presence, watching the neighborhoods he'd planned for tonight. So his plans changed--he was prepared enough to have alternatives--and he'd packed up to leave as soon as the evening's shopping--and post-shopping--festivities were done. Now, dusk had chased the sun close to the horizon and, from his perch on the driveway, he watched the evening's offerings parade past his candy bowl.

The evening had crept on, slowly, but inevitably, toward what George thought of as prime shopping time. The crowds dwindled even more, but George was intimately aware of every remaining child on his street. A noisy group of junior high school boys came up his drive, dressed in only the most cursory of costumes. Clearly, they were too old for trick-or-treating, but not too old to turn their backs on free candy. Each carried an over-laden pillow case that they presented to him, in turn.

"Evening, boys!" George said. "Pretty good haul so far, huh?"

"Yeah," they answered in unison, looking knowingly at each other. "Real good!"

George found himself wondering, as he dropped a piece of candy in each of their pillowcases, how many younger kids had donated their night's earnings to these guys. He couldn't help noticing the irony: Halloween brought out the predator in people.

"Behave, boys!" he called after them. They were already gone, laughing and pushing each other as they disappeared into the night.

Minutes passed before the next visitor came. A little girl made her way up the driveway toward him. She was wearing a white, robe-like dress with what appeared to be homemade wings fixed to the back. An angel. Maybe a fairy. The cheap mask on her face featured a halo--definitely an angel.

And she was alone.

George scanned up and down the block. There wasn't a single car on the street and, as far as he could see, there weren't any other children either. He did a quick check of the houses around him. Most had already turned off their lights and, with the trees on his property, his neighbors couldn't see him at his front porch even if they were looking. Opportunities blossomed in his mind.

Well, well, well. Looks like I'll be staying in tonight.

The girl stopped in front of him and waited expectantly. George put on his friendly face.

"Oooh, look at you! Aren't you just the prettiest thing? Would you like some candy?"

The girl regarded him through the eyeholes of her mask for a moment before giving a quick nod. George rose out of his seat and took a step toward the front door.

"Okay, so I have some real special candy in the house that I save just for little girls *just* like you. Come up here."

He was ready to grab her and bolt for the door in case she showed signs of reluctance -- no telling how long the street would remain this empty -- but the girl followed him obediently. He turned to open the screen door.

"It's just in the other room. If you wanna come in, I'll get it for..."

When he turned back to see if the girl was stupid enough to go inside with him, he saw that she had been joined by another trick-or-treater. This one was a little boy, perhaps a year older than her but it was hard to tell. He was wearing one of those elongated ghoul masks made popular by that slasher flick a few years ago.

"Oh! I didn't hear you come up, son. You gave me quite a start!"

George scanned the street again and once more, he saw no sign of anyone.

Two for the price of one?

The idea was powerfully exciting to him, but even so, he was a little worried. George considered himself to be a cautious collector -- careful enough that, as far as he knew, he had never been a suspect in any of the child disappearances and murders that he had committed over the course of his life. That cautious part of him was telling him that it was damn strange how this cute little girl showed up at his doorstep, unescorted and unwatched. Stranger still that the boy would show up the same way. Something didn't smell right about the whole deal, but he sure as hell couldn't see what it was.

And they were *so* close to being inside...

He held open the door for them and they filed into the house. Following behind, he kicked the front door halfway closed and stepped around them so he could get into the kitchen.

"Just a second, kids, the good stuff's here in the kitchen."

George kept a container of acetone under the kitchen sink. It wasn't quite as effective as chloroform but it was easier to buy and more importantly, tucked in with all his cleaning supplies, so it didn't look out of place. It was also easy for him to quickly pull out the container and soak a dish rag -- which he did -- making sure that the center of rag was good and saturated. He grabbed an extra bag of candy he'd left on the counter, holding it in one hand and the acetone-soaked rag slightly behind his back.

He rounded the corner from the kitchen into the entryway, wearing his most winning smile, surprised to see *three* kids.

Another girl had joined the first two. She was, perhaps, eleven or twelve and a head taller than them. She had dressed up something like Catwoman, with the cat ears and tail, along with a black mask covering her eyes. Her face, however, was done up in pale, flat makeup that didn't go along with the costume.

George decided on the spot to abandon his plan. He was terribly disappointed, but the cautious voice that had carried him so far was now practically screaming that he was being set up for something. George was inclined to believe it. He tucked the rag into his back pocket.

"Where'd you come from, honey?" he asked the new arrival, his smile fading a bit. "You weren't here before."

That twinge of wrongness was joined by a flicker of fear, fluttering in his stomach. This was odd. Pretty fucking odd, at that. He decided that it was time for these kids to leave. As soon as possible.

"So who wants candy? Open up those bags!"

George grabbed a handful of chocolate bars and leaned down to the little girl.

"I believe you were first," he told her.

He started to drop one of the candy bars into her sack, then recoiled. Something was moving inside. Something writhing. A lot of somethings writhing.

"JEEZ! What th'..."

George jumped back and stumbled over two boys, dressed almost identically in some kind of creepy-looking skeleton outfits as the earlier boy. Somehow they had slipped into the house and positioned themselves behind him. George might have fallen had they not stepped out of the way at the last second. He took a couple of clumsy steps and, by the time he had regained his balance, there were two more children standing in a group with the rest. All of the kids were holding out their bags and walking toward him.

George did not want to see what was in their bags.

He backed into the kitchen and the children followed. Given enough room, he might have continued backing indefinitely, afraid to show his back to the children who were already there, afraid even more that additional children would be waiting behind him. But he could not continue backing up--he hit the refrigerator on the far wall. Nowhere left to go. The number of children had grown again and they surrounded him.

"W-what d'you kids want? Get out of here!!"

From the front of the ring of children surrounding George, the first little girl stepped forward and showed him her open bag. Maggots squirmed inside, crawling over each in endless motion. Raising a hand, she pulled the mask from her face.

"No!"

Under the mask, most of the girl's face was gone, eaten away by decay, by the grave, by the maggots which were wriggling out of a dozen places and dropping into the bag she held.

"God, no!"

Even though her face was ravaged, somehow George recognized her. One of his victims from a past Halloween. Of course he knew her--how could he not? Not now that she'd shown him her face. He'd spent a lot of time with this girl before she died.

He saw her clearly now. Her arms were mostly bones, with the last few clumps of skin hanging off in rags. Her costume robe was a funeral dress, stained with dirt and slimed green with mold. Lank strands of dark hair straggled down over her shoulders. And her eyes.

They were empty sockets that somehow still burned with an intensity that was terrifying to look at.

When she turned those eyes up to George and smiled, he felt a piece of his sanity slip.

"Trick or treat," she said in a voice that sounded like the grave.

Then she snatched a piece of flesh from his leg, dropped it in her bag, and turned to walk out the front door. George screamed and clutched at the wound, blood spilling between his fingers.

The little boy pushed his way through the children and removed his mask. Underneath, his face was mostly skull, jaw hanging crookedly and his exposed teeth looking unnaturally long and dangerous. A bit of a gristle from his nose and a few tufts of once-blond hair were all that was left of what once was a handsome young boy. George remembered him, nonetheless. Remembered what he'd done to the boy. Remembered how he'd killed him.

The boy held open his bag, showing George a tangle of intestines though which something large and odd-shaped seemed to be passing, back and forth. Whatever was in there was alive. George retched at the sight of it, but he couldn't look away.

The boy stepped closer, a hand now caressing George's hand and the fist-sized hole in his blood-soaked thigh. George started whimpering as the boy's fingers walked playfully toward his genitals and he began pleading with the boy, louder as his hand got closer to its intended target: "No, *don't*. no...no...No...NO...NOOOOO!!"

he boy ripped off George's testicles--tearing through his trousers and underwear--and dropped them into his bag with a meaty thud. Like the girl before him, the boy turned and walked out of the house, leaving George slid to the floor, howling in agony.

The other children took their turns, one by one, standing before their killer, showing them what they had brought in their bags, and removing their mask so that he could know them. One by one, they collected their treat and departed.

Eventually George fell silent, clinging above whatever abyss awaited him by only the thinnest of threads. A solitary girl was all that remained. She stood for a moment over what was left of him--her Catwoman mask dangling from one hand and her bag bulging oddly at the item she had chosen to take from his body.

She stood there a long time, watching the light fade from George's eyes before she, too, walked to the front door, pausing only to turn off the porch light before fading into the darkness beyond.

# Masklore
## Michael H. Hanson

"The human face is, after all, nothing more nor less than a mask." – Agatha Christie

*Masklore*'s proprietress, a tall, slender, beautiful redhead of indeterminate age, considers the offer from the handsome young black man standing opposite to her from across the glass sales counter, a solid clear plexiglass screen fully separating them.

*Wearing a Mask*, by the Ducktails, plays from four overhead speakers.

"A thousand, cash," Daniel says again. "Check the bills, Ariadne, they're clean."

She ponders the offer and the object, a beautiful, full multicolor Tlingit shaman mask originally carved in wood and painted in a small tribal coastal region in Alaska. She acquired it for a mere one hundred dollars and a personal favor, a steal really, and she weighs its true secret innate value.

"Fifteen hundred, then," Daniel adds, "and not a penny more. We got a deal?"

"Your charms don't work on me, pretty boy lawyer," Adriadne smirks as her pale green eyes glint, "you're not counting the high-end CDC-approved face filter custom install… two thousand smackeroos or you can hit the bricks."

Daniel shoves his right hand into the backside of his tight-fitting Brunello Cusinelli single-breasted blazer, pulls out a small wad of twenties and slams them on the counter, right in front of the small opening at the base of the transparent barrier.

"Deal," he says, "and put it in your sturdiest box."

A few minutes later and Daniel's frown returns to a smile. He stops and turns around after opening the front door.

"You always were a shrewd negotiator, Ariadne," he says, "Happy Halloween!"

"Happy Halloween," she replies.

Halloween is, in fact, still a full two nights away. But the recent spike in business just before the second Halloween following the original Covid-19 outbreak leaves Ariadne little time for sleep. This sixth wave of the corona virus is a curse on the public, but ironically a godsend to a business that centers on unusual merchandise. Contemporary yet authentic tribal masks from all over the world custom fitted with top of the line N95 filters. For every person that finds them garish and macabre, someone else delights in their otherworldly allure. And with an upcoming night of Trick or Treating with the kids, or adult gatherings for various parties, Masklore's masks are back in hot demand.

Ariadne remembers when she first opened the shop, roughly one month before that first Halloween during the 2020 viral outbreak. A lot of companies had gone out of business by this time and it was no problem finding a decent-sized workplace for a cheap price with lots of shelf space in Hidden Lake, Colorado, not quite a village and generally referred to as a Census-Designated Place with its sub-forty population.

103

Masklore sits on a lone empty stretch of Pine Cone Circle and is a large traditionally built log cabin, once home to a family of nine. Hanging from the lower edge of the front roof is a massive bronze replica of a traditional Benin ivory West African Mask. It represents the Queen Mother Idia, fabricated in secret by Nigerian sculptor Erhabor Ogieva Emokpae in nineteen eighty-two. It was three feet tall and weighed at least four hundred and ninety pounds. Beneath it is a large green and white sign sporting the shop's name in ornate Celtic style letters. No potential customer ever drives past this store unawares.

Ariadne's Colorado clientele actually like that her place is mostly off the beaten path. Its odd location only adds to the mystery and contemporary mythos of her establishment. Ariadne's special top quality authentic tribal masks are rumored on occasion to possess supernatural nuances. Nothing clearly defined or predictable in any manner but strange things seem to happen in their vicinity, or so it is whispered between confidantes late at night.

One mumbled tale holds that a woman wearing a large female African PWEVO mask fought off an assault by her enraged drunken husband in their large, expensive home on the end of Kalmia Drive in Boulder, CO. When the police arrived an hour later after neighbors reported hearing a series of terrifying screams, all they found was a crying wife sitting on a couch next to a weird tribal mask. The husband had apparently run off, but had done so on foot, not taking anything at all with him, not even his prized Rolls Royce car. One officer reported being slightly creeped out by a weird six-foot-tall tree sculpture in a corner of the living room that vaguely reminded him of a person crouching down in agony.

Another campfire tale stated that one of Ariadne's ancient silver Persian war masks had been purchased by a teenage boy who had been bullied quite regularly in his hometown of Lafayette since Kindergarten. Rumor held that a half a dozen football jocks had cornered him on the backside of the Seven Eleven store and attacked him. The bullies had been reported missing a few days later and somehow, some way, authorities in Tehran, Iran reported the apprehension and imprisonment of six American male spies near one of their government buildings. They were apparently repatriated over a year later after a series of personal secret payments from the boys' parents.

The apparent folktales increased over time, though of course nothing that ever makes the local TV news nor appears in any legitimate newspaper, magazine, or online blog.

Whatever the truth, Masklore's high prices do not seem to turn away or offend the majority of her customers at this time of year. Ariadne is down to roughly seventy-five percent of her stock with thirty-five hours until All Hallows Eve. She hopes she has enough left for what she sees coming… a riotous run on her remaining product line.

\*\*\*

The next day Ariadne calls in all five of her part-time employees because the shop is figuratively being assaulted by frenzied customers crowding together in a long, zig-zagging outdoor line stretching down the road and out of sight. Only ten are being allowed in the store at any time and three rapidly emptying boxes of medical masks wait on a table just outside the front door. Inside, pushy customers press up against the three sides of the U-shaped display counters. Ariadne purchased an expensive air purification system a year ago, consisting of ten blowers with five filtration units all humming loudly in the surrounding walls. Containers of antiseptic gel lay atop counters every five feet.

Rise Against's *Black Mask and Gasoline* starts blaring from the overhead speakers when a bright blue wig catches Ariadne's attention and she shouts, "Skaði, over here." Moments later a tall slim woman about six feet tall, yet still shorter than Masklore's owner, moves forward and steps behind the counter carrying a large box.

"I hope this is what I think it is, Skaði," Ariadne smiles.

"One dozen woven Indian tribal masks from Panama, as promised," Skaði replies in a surprisingly deep voice.

Ariadne swipes Skaði's InstaBag credit card and returns her receipt, along with a healthy cash tip.

"If you need anything else," Skaði says with a smile, "you know I shop and deliver at all hours."

106

"Which is why I always ask for you, young lady," Ariadne laughs. "Say, I love that new eyeshadow you're wearing. What's it called?"

"I used the Mothership V: Bronze Seduction Palette from Pat McGrath Labs," she replies, "and yes, it is to die for."

"So, the surgery is soon?"

"Well," Skaði says, "I decided to get my Adam's apple shaved first, then after full recovery I'll go under the knife for the big procedure."

Ariadne reaches forward and the two bump fists.

"Girl power," they say in unison and laugh.

"Got another delivery," Skaði says, starting to turn away. "Catch you on the flipside…"

"Not before I get my joke," Ariadne shouts.

"Oh, right," Skaði stops in her tracks, "ummm… Wear a mask before seeing posts that are trending… because they are viral."

Ariadne groans loudly and the two ladies wave goodbye as Eminem's *Ski Mask Way* starts playing.

Over the next hour Ariadne sells three paper maché Rapa Nui masks, five Mexican Day of The Dead masks, one Chinese New Year's mask, six African Fatima masks and a whopping ten Austrian Krampusnacht festival masks. None of the customers seem to care about the backstories and original purposes of these works of art. They just want something to wear for a variety of adult parties they are attending Halloween night. Most admit to plans for attending festivities in either Denver or Boulder.

"Ariadne," one of her workers yells from across the shop, "do we do trades?"

The shop owner frowns and walks around the perimeter of the counter as Tiffany Dawn's *Mask* plays from the overhead speakers. Her employee, Bobby, a twenty-year-old Asian-American junior from the University of Colorado at Boulder, is standing across from and looking at a solid middle-aged man of average height wearing a pale white suit and sporting a head of long brown hair combed straight back. He is clean shaven and has a Mediterranean cast about him.

"Guy here says he's got something special you'd be interested in, boss," Bobby says.

"Right," Ariadne replies, "I'll take care of this. Go into the storage room and grab some Philippine demon masks to restock the side display shelves."

"You got it boss," Bobby says, frowning at the strange man before leaving.

*The Mask*, by the Fugees, begins playing from the speakers

"It's been decades, Abraxas," Ariadne says, "and I heard a rumor that you were taken out by that explosion in Beirut awhile back."

"To quote Mister Twain," Abraxas smiles, "the rumors of my death have been greatly exaggerated."

Abraxas' lips split for a moment, revealing a mouth packed with bright white teeth, with the single exception of his right fang tooth which had a shiny ruby imbedded in it.

"You sure don't look any the worse for wear," Ariadne says. "In fact, you don't look like you've aged a day in half a century."

"Look who's talking," Abraxas replies. "I'd say among Centenarians, you are certainly a spring chicken, Ariadne. Now, to business."

Abraxas reaches into his large satchel and pulls out a long, hand-carved wood mask.

"Bob Marley's personal tribal Jamaican mask," Abraxas says, "which he wore only once at the Maroon festival, about a year before his death."

Ariadne's eyes go wide.

"Your reputation is above reproach, Abraxas," she says slowly, "but I'm not sure you can put a price on this."

"I have it on good authority you've got the very first prototype Dark Vader mask, fabricated by Brian Muir himself, locked away in your safe."

"A plight on your dark soul," Ariadne scowls.

"Fair trade?" Abraxas asks.

"Fair trade," she replies and they each spit into their right hands before slapping them together in a tight handshake.

Five minutes later, a brown paper wrapped bundle under his right arm, Abraxas turns to leave but stops for a moment to glare at Ariadne with his shining yellow eyes.

"You seem unnaturally calm, especially considering the times."

"What?" Ariadne shrugs. "I caught Covid twice and I'm still standing."

"That's not what I meant," Abraxas says, raising his eyebrow dramatically.

"Then what are you…"

Abraxas strains his neck, twisting his head almost one hundred and eighty degrees to look up the high wall of the rear most part of the display room. Ariadne follows his gaze and her eyes rest upon a large mask and head-covering, deer antlers jutting from it, perched near the top of the ceiling's arch.

"I hope you slept well last night," Abraxas says from behind her, "you'll certainly need all your strength come midnight."

"Hey," Ariadne says, spinning around, but too late to catch Abraxas, who has somehow slipped away and disappeared from the shop like an invisible wraith.

Ariadne pulls back the left sleeve of her thick blue and green Aran island sweater. The green and black tattoo near the base of her forearm, displaying the symbol of The Awen, is pulsing with green light.

"A 'Cho-fharpais agus an Dùbhlan," she speaks in a harsh but almost silent whisper in ancient Celtic. "How did I miss you?"

Graham Parker's *Under The Mask of Happiness* starts playing from the speakers.

\*\*\*

The shop closes at eleven twenty pm. Ariadne shoves the front door shut and closes the door latch as Fleetwood Mac's *Behind The Mask* started playing from the overhead speakers.

"That was intense," Debbie says, another university of Colorado student some of her other employees had brought on this Fall Semester to earn a little under-the-counter double-overtime money.

"Bobby, Debbie, Melpomene and Frank," Ariadne says with a smile. "Here is your pay with a nice Halloween bonus," shoving the wads of cash into the welcome young hands. "Now you four go home. Iostha and I will clean up. Now get!"

A minute later Ariadne turns to her remaining employee, the oldest of the five, a native-American woman of Mohawk descent who stands almost five foot eleven and built like an Olympic swimmer.

"What's the matter, Ariadne?" Iostha asks. "You've been pensive ever since that muscular guy in the white suit arrived earlier."

"It is time, Iostha," Ariadne speaks formally. "The challenge will begin shortly, at midnight."

Iostha gasps and then looks up at the wall clock. It read eleven forty-five pm.

"I've trained you for five years," Ariadne says, "and I…"

"I'm ready, my Tidsear Banrigh," Iostha says with a slight bow.

"No," Ariadne replies with a sad smile, "you are not. But you shall be my witness and if I should fall, you will take up my cause in future years. Now, we have but minutes to prepare for the ritual. Help me move everything off the main floor and the countertops."

\*\*\*

111

The ancient eighteenth century standing Irish clock starts chiming as Ariadne and Iostha finish placing the last of the green granite stones inscribed with esoteric runes around the periphery of the main floor.

Upon the twelfth chime, two columns of smoke, one green, one purple, slowly appear. Ariadne rests easy as she remembered to tell Iostha to turn off all the smoke and fire detectors. If any incendiary disasters occur, they will be ones initiated by those present.

A minute later the colored smokes dissipate and reveal the presence of four people. Close to the entrance is a large Asian woman, as tall as Ariadne. Next to her is a shorter young man who looked Russian.

"Hail, Nuwa," Ariadne says. "You honor my home."

"This is Dima," Nuwa says in idiomatic English with the slightest Cantonese accent. "He is my second."

Ariadne turns to her right to acknowledge a lovely tall woman of African descent built like a gymnast and whose head is shaved. This lack of mane in no way takes away from her countenance which radiates both nobility and beauty. Standing beside her is a young woman of East Indian descent, wearing a bright yellow Sari.

"Welcome, Minona," Ariadne says with a smile. "Peace be with you."

"This is Fulki," Minona says. "She is my second."

Ariadne gestures toward her employee. "This is Iostha, my second."

"You are the host," Minona says plainly. "The words are yours."

Ariadne walks around to the rear of the main sales counter. Everyone else steps back, to press against the long stretches of counter along the two sides of the shop.

"This is the challenge of destiny," Ariadne begins, "which was chosen by our ancestors to determine the path of human fate for every generation."

"This is the challenge," Minona and Nuwa say in unison.

"We are the avatars of the three paths," Ariadne says, "I am Nature, Minona is Humanity and Nuwa is Dream."

"We are the avatars," Minona and Nuwa reply.

"Let the battle commence," Ariadne says.

Instantly, Iostha, Fulki and Dima walk around behind the long counter as Nuwa and Minona stride to the center of the floor.

Ariadne sighs, knowing this ancient altercation is nothing so pithy as a power struggle between *Good* and *Evil*, nor as unimaginative as a contest between *Science* and *Magic*. No, this ritual will strain the boundaries between slightly less fundamental esoteric foundations of reality as it is currently perceived here on Earth.

Ariadne steps around her sales counter and out onto the main floor with a bag clutched in her right hand. In moments, she and her two guests form the points of a triangle.

Instantly, the Celtic stones surrounding the main floor suddenly light up, the outlines of the ancient lettering inscribed in them glow brightly as a mostly transparent sparkling veil appears to rise from the floor, separating the three women from the rest of the shop.

Simultaneously the three ladies each reach into their bags and pull out tribal masks from various ancient cultures around the world.

Nuwa removes an eleventh century BC Chinese Bronze Sanxingdui mask with a stern countenance whose guise is still mostly covered with a thin gold veneer. She slowly presses it to her face and then carefully ties together the new nylon straps attached to it, behind her head. Her long black hair spills around and under it like an ebony waterfall.

Minona removes an ornate one-thousand-year-old Mwaash aMbooy mask of the Kuba people. It is a fierce façade made of leopard and antelope skin with nose and ears carved from wood. The fact that by tradition it is only to be worn by kings or chiefs shows Minona's disdain for the temporal laws of men. She raises it quickly then slowly lowers it upon her smooth shaved head.

Ariadne pulls out an eleven-thousand-year-old Mesolithic deer skull headdress mask and slowly places it atop her head, her long flowing red hair splays out beneath it like a living extension of her will. The ornamental headgear with its long antlers gives her countenance an arcane and potent aspect.

"Ràng tā kāishǐ," Nuwa shouts in Chinese Mandarin.

"Acha ianze," Minona yells in Swahili.

"Leig leis tòiseachadh," Ariadne joins in, speaking Gaelic.

Instantly, the eye holes in Nuwa's mask glow with a pulsing blue light, those in Minona's mask flash with a blood red bubbling glow and Ariadne's mask exudes a bright green incandescence that swirls like smoke.

Nuwa's green slacks and grey Nehru jacket flash out of existence and are instantly replaced by a brilliant blue robe. Minona's brown leather culotte suit turns into a tight, single-piece leopard pattern dress. Adriadne looks down and sees her sweater and blue jeans morph into a long green wool cloak.

"My will has ruled the last century," Minona says, her voice sounding louder than any human can talk or yell, her eyes flashing red, "and several before it. Humanity has progressed in numbers and culture and technology and lusts. Retreat now and there will be no repercussions."

"Precious species die every year," Ariadne speaks, her own voice also raises up like it is spewing from a rock concert set of speakers, her eyes glowing green, "the oceans, forests, jungles, mountains, lakes, rivers and deserts suffer poisonous pollution and the air grows foul. Your reign is failure. I will not back down."

"You are both fools," Nuwa says, her loud echoing voice making the glass on the sales counter shake and ring, her eyes continuing to pulse with a blue light. "You each treasure the temporal, the present, the rational, the substance of life, atoms,

115

touch, rain, sun, wind, the scream of hawk and jaguar, the splash of blood on lips and teeth… it is all one thing and it is meaningless. The world is a dream within a dream. If you could but release your strangleholds on your delusions, you would understand… and no, I will not surrender to either of you this time. I will no longer declare my neutrality as I did so many times before. This world deserves more than your two narrow views."

Twin beams of colored light fly from their three sets of eyes and intersected between them. The triple splash of brilliant light blinds their three observers on the periphery for a full thirty seconds.

In moments, a globe of boiling multi-colored fires like a small sun is born in the air between the three combatants. It slowly grows from the size of a baseball to that of a large pumpkin as it levitates, constantly being fed by six beams of energy. As dramatic a visage as this creation is, no actual heat seems to emanate from it.

The flow of green light doubles from Ariadne's eyes and a loud growl escapes her lips. "We must return to the ancient Shamanism. We must replace science with Animism."

The colorful globe of fire overhead slowly turns a bright green as Ariadne talks. Nuwa and Minona's eye beams grow thinner and fainter and they both groan in pain.

"No," Minona shouts, "the world is and always will be a wasteland. It is humanity that gives this planet any and all meaning. My rationalism is our only future."

116

Just then Minona's twin beams of light grow much brighter and the globe overhead turns mostly scarlet.

"Release your fears and desires," Nuwa yells. "You both grasp for self-destructive absolutes that will annihilate reality itself over time." Just then the blue beams of light from her eyes grow three times as bright as the overhead burning globe next turns blue.

"I will not yield," Minona says in rabid desperation.

"I will not yield," Ariadne says maniacally.

The large globe begins pulsing like a giant heart and with each expansion and contraction, the inner walls of Masklore begin creaking and finally flexing. Cracks start appearing across the long glass countertop and across all the surrounding windows. Masklore appears to be on the verge of exploding from within.

Iostha, Fulki, and Dima cower behind the nearby counter, frightened of the fantastic powers on display and terrified by the fact that their tutors are seemingly unwilling to compromise their beliefs and desires.

"Your arrogance would destroy us, our apprentices, this entire state and eventually the entire solar system" Nuwa says. "Thus I must break this stalemate, for the good of all."

"Mistress, no," Dima shouts from the sidelines, but it is too late.

Nuwa's entire body begins to glow with the same blue energy that came from her eyes. The globe overhead doubles in size and its sides almost touch the surrounding walls.

The entire building starts shaking. The thin spectral veil surrounding the main floor begins to swirl and flash in a wide variety of colors.

"Jiéshù!" Nuwa screams in Chinese just before the fiery globe explodes and blinds everyone.

***

Sometime later, perhaps a minute, perhaps an hour, no one can tell, everyone comes to their senses and stands up. There are only five people in the shop. Nuwa is nowhere to be seen. The fiery globe has disappeared and there is no sign of scorching or burning anywhere. The earlier cracks in the counter and the windows have disappeared. Nothing seems out of place.

Minona and Ariadne remove their masks.

"There has never been such an outcome before," Minona says.

"The fires did not accept my claim either," Ariadne says, "but by dying and incorporealizing, I think Nuwa's claim is also rejected."

"Does this mean the current balance of power will remain the same until the next challenge?" Minona asks.

"Or perhaps the fates will roll their dice and make a random choice," Ariadne replies. "Only time will tell."

Minona nods, gestures her second, Fulki, to her side.

"In another generation, my sisters," Minona say, and then, in a splash of red light, she and her assistant disappear.

Ariadne looks sadly at Nuwa's second, Dima, who seems distraught while holding Nuwa's fallen mask in his hands.

"She finished training you, apprentice?" Ariadne asks.

"Yes," Dima says, letting out a long breath. "She prepared me for this long ago. I will not let her down."

"Then… until the next time, brother," Ariadne says.

"Yes," Dima replies. "I will return." He disappears in a bright splash of blue light.

Iostha walks up to an exhausted Ariadne who hands over the ancient deer skull headdress.

"Return this to its honored place upon the wall, Iostha," Ariadne says.

"What do you really think this outcome bodes, my mistress?"

"Minona's reign of cold human rationalism is coming to an end," Ariadne replies.

"Then, Nature will finally ascend?" Iostha gasps.

"No," Ariadne shakes her head, "nothing so arbitrarily absolute. But, I believe for the first time since man stood upright there will now be a true balance… maybe even a fusion of dream, nature and humanity… possibly enough to start cleansing this planet of its poisons and killings."

"And Nuwa's dream?" Iostha asks.

"Perhaps *it* is the mask that we will all now place upon the face of reality."

# Night of the Goblins
## Kevin Jones

The engine sputtered then died altogether. Dominick pounded his fist on the steering wheel as he pulled to the side of the road. Eva's eyelids fluttered before opening. "What's the matter, baby, did this old piece of junk breakdown again? I've told you a million times you should get a new car! Why don't you ever listen to me?"

Dominick gave a flustered sigh. "First of all we're not broken down, the car's only stalled. I'll get it started again and second, I wouldn't sell this car even if someone offered me a million bucks for it. It's a classic."

He turned the key in the ignition over and over again but nothing happened. The engine did not show the faintest hint of life. When Dominick rubbed his hand against his forehead he saw it was smeared with the white vampire makeup Eva had painstakingly applied to his face earlier in the evening. "You know, I'm really starting to feel like an idiot all dressed up in this dime store costume you made me wear to Rachel's Halloween party. I mean, the whole thing was just stupid, a bunch of grownups acting like two year olds. How dumb can you get?"

Eva crossed her legs and playfully fingered one of her large gold earrings, "What's the matter, sweetheart, don't you like my nurse's costume?"

"Well, to be perfectly honest the only thing I still enjoy about Halloween is that it gives hot girls

121

a chance to dress sleazy. The rest of it is a bunch of moronic nonsense."

Eva yawned wearily. "So how are we going to get home, do you want me to call a cab?"

Dominick shot her a dirty look. "What do we need a cab for? Just give me a second and I'll get this baby up and running in no time."

A bitterly cold breeze sent a shiver up Dominick's spine as he got out of the car. He propped up the hood and started to check the engine, then began to notice something strange. It was only a little after eleven o'clock but the streets seemed utterly deserted. There wasn't another car or Halloween reveler in sight. Dominick shook his head in disgust. The engine looked fine. He muttered angrily to himself. "Okay, so why won't you start?"

It wasn't the idea of trying to get a cab or going through the hassle of having his car towed back to his place that was upsetting him; it was admitting defeat in front of Eva. He knew she would give him the business about this for days. For some strange reason she hated his old Trans Am and was always trying to make him sell his most treasured possession. Dominick was about to take one last stab at getting the engine to turn over when he heard a strange scurrying noise behind him. When he turned around he thought he'd see a stray dog or an alley cat but what was before him was far more bizarre. A three-foot robed figure stood on the sidewalk.

Dominick chuckled nervously. "Jesus, kid, you startled me. Don't you think it's a little late to be trick or treating?"

The diminutive, hooded stranger did not reply. Dominick began to grow more and more impatient by the second as he growled. "Well, are you just going to stand there like some kind of a creep staring at me all night or what? If you want any candy, kid, you're out of luck because I don't got any."

The tiny hooded lurker raised a clawed hand covered in short black coarse hair and pointed at Dominick's gold watch. "Christ, kid, you must be some kind of a frigging nut! I'm not gonna give you my watch. The only way you're gonna get it is if you pry it off my cold dead hand!"

Eva honked the horn impatiently as she called out the window. "Is this old rust bucket going to start or not? I'd like to get home some time tonight, you know."

In the few seconds that it had taken Dominick to glare back at his girlfriend and tell her to quit wailing on the horn, the beggar had vanished. After hurriedly closing the hood, Dominick slid behind the wheel. No matter how many times he turned the key the engine would not start. Eva was about to make another glib remark but the words died on her lips as the tiny prankster jumped up onto the hood. She clutched Dominick's costume sleeve fearfully as she whispered. "What the hell is this kid's problem? Is he high on drugs or something?"

"I don't know but he's going to get his head broke if he's scratched my car." Steam nearly shot

123

out of Dominick's ears as he leapt from the car. "Get off of my goddamned hood, you little punk, before I beat your ass!"

The trickster let out a low rumbling chuckle and started to jump up and down, badly denting the metal beneath his tiny feet. Dominick grabbed the vandal by his robe. A low terrified moan escaped his lips as the nightmare thing's hood fell back. It was not a child at all; it did not even appear to be human. The creature's eyes were a horrid crimson; they sat above an upturned pig's snout and a mouth full of jagged razor sharp teeth. The green skinned beast reared back its tiny, clawed hand and viciously slashed at Dominick's face. Three deep gashes ran down the length of his cheek. Blood poured like an open faucet onto the front of his white shirt. He hurled the monster to the pavement and stomped its head in with his heavy work boots. Florescent yellow blood dripped down into the gutter as the goblin emitted its death rattle.

Eva rushed to her boyfriend's aid. She pressed a handful of tissues that she had scrounged from her purse to his cheek. "What the hell is that thing, Dominick?"

"How should I know? I've never seen anything like it."

"These cuts look really deep I think you're going to have to go to the hospital. Do you want me to call an ambulance?"

Dominick nodded slightly. "Yeah, that's probably a good idea but let's do it somewhere else, we need to be with people."

The terrified couple hurried down the dark empty street in search of refuge. All the while they could hear scurrying sounds and tiny feet pounding the pavement behind them. Up ahead they could see a light, a Mexican fast food restaurant with a drive-thru still open. Eva ran ahead and banged on the door. "Hello in there, somebody please help us! My boyfriend's been hurt! Let us in."

A high school kid with shaggy red hair and a face covered with freckles appeared at the counter. "I'm sorry, the dining area is closed, you'll have to go to the drive-thru."

"Jesus Christ, kid, I don't want a freaking taco! My boyfriend's hurt and someone's after us. You have to let us in!"

He looked past Eva and saw Dominick staggering towards them, a handful of bloody tissues clutched to his cheek. "Okay, hold on one second, I'll open the door. "

The young man hopped over the counter with a set of keys in his hand. Eva scrambled inside, then heard Dominick cry out in pain. She turned and saw what was happening to her boyfriend. All the color drained from her face. Dominick rolled and thrashed on the ground as several tiny, cloaked creatures, identical to the one that had attacked them, were mugging him. him. One of the monsters gave a triumphant squeal as it yanked off Dominick's watch.

Eva tried to go to Dominick's aid but the employee grabbed her and pulled her into the restaurant. While he fumbled with his keys, desperately trying to get the door locked, he whispered fearfully. "What in God's name are those things?"

Eva spun around and shot him a withering look. "You open that door right now, you little son of a bitch!"

"Forget it, lady! Look, your boyfriend's already stopped moving, I think he's dead."

The world seemed to slow to a crawl as Eva turned. Dominick's still form lay in the parking lot, his clothes torn into rags and blood pouring freely on to the blacktop. The goblins began to drag Dominick's body into the shadows. The horrid creatures seemed to melt away into the night but Eva knew they were still out there, watching and waiting. Eva felt numb all over. "We have to call an ambulance."

The kid pulled his phone from his pocket. "What the hell, it's dead. This is crazy; I charged it before I left for work. Try yours."

Eva dumped the contents of her purse onto a nearby dining table and realised her phone was missing. "I must have left it back at the car."

"It's okay, I'll use the landline in the kitchen." He vanished behind the counter. A few seconds later she heard a string of obscenities. He ran back out front. "I don't believe it, that one's dead too. What the hell's going on?"

Eva yelped as the lights went out. Tears ran down her cheeks as she sobbed. "This can't be happening, this is a nightmare, any minute now I'm going to wake up and be safe in bed."

"Just try to calm down. We'll figure a way out of this. Say, I don't think we've been properly introduced. My name's Joe, what's your name?"

"Eva, my name's Eva."

"You're safe now, Eva, the restaurant's locked up; those things can't get in here."

Eva wiped tears from her eyes and murmured softly. "I wouldn't be so sure about that, Joe. Those goblins or whatever they are have some kind of powers. The phones won't work, the lights are out and where is everybody? That's a busy street and it's Halloween night, for Christ's sake. It's still early; there should be tons of people out partying."

"Look, Eva, I don't know what's going on but I'm sure it's not some kind of black magic. There's got to be a logical explanation. We'll be safe if we just stay locked in here. You'll see, someone will come to the drive-thru and we'll have them call for help."

Hour after hour passed and still no help arrived. The world outside remained strangely quiet, nothing moved anywhere. To the besieged people occupying the restaurant it felt as if they were the last man and woman on Earth. Near dawn, Joe let out an exuberant whoop that roused Eva from her fitful slumber. Headlights were approaching the restaurant.

Joe grinned from ear to ear. "Holy crap, that's a cop car and it's heading straight for the drive-thru." He tossed Eva the keys. "You let him in after I tell the cop what's going on."

HE turned and ran towards the kitchen. When the police car pulled up to the drive-thru window the smile quickly evaporated. The cop was dead. He had been slashed to pieces by dozens of tiny, clawed hands. In the corpse's lap sat one of the minuscule robed goblins, on the floor another one of the creatures manipulated the pedals. Joe let out one last terrified scream as the horrid monsters leapt from the car and tore into his flesh.

Eva trembled uncontrollably as she called out," Joe? What's happening? Are you all right?"

A pair of little red eyes peeked over the counter, followed by another then another. Eva tried to make her badly shaking hand force the key into the front door lock as the goblins bounded over the counter and scrambled towards her. When the nightmarish creatures were mere inches from her legs she finally managed to get the door open.

The hysterical young woman sprinted into the parking lot and kept running until her lungs burned. Throughout her panicked flight she could hear the goblins nipping at her heels. Just when her strength had about given out, the sun started to peek over the horizon. A thought flashed through Eva's mind, it must be her gold ear rings the goblins were after. She tore them off and threw them on the ground.

The whole neighborhood started to shimmer as Eva began to hear the sounds of car engines, dogs barking and birds singing in the trees. Eva ran out into the street and felt the dawn's first orange rays on her face.

When she turned she saw that the goblins had stopped their pursuit. The horrid little monsters lurked in the mouth of a shadowy alley and whispered excitedly amongst themselves as they scooped up their prize. The ground began to tremble and a fissure opened in the blacktop. The creatures let out a series of snarls and hisses before they crawled into the opening and vanished deep into the bowels of the earth with their treasure. For the rest of her life, on October 31$^{St}$ Eva would shut herself up in her home and not let anyone come within a thousand feet of her who was wearing anything made out of gold.

# Once In A Blue Moon
## Diane Arrelle

Gerald, who had just turned seventeen, set up the sound system, stringing the speakers on top of the flat roofs of the mausoleums. He saw several adults from the caravan bring out tables and chairs. They spaced them around the grassy circle where the streets spoked off to the four corners of the cemetery.

Gerald nodded and shouted to them, "This is going to be the best party. Ever!"

"Yes," Misty, who was almost twenty, said as she walked up behind him. "The best."

"It's been, like, years and I sure could use the exercise," he added. "I haven't seen any people from town in at least a century."

Two more people joined the conversation. "Gerald, stop exaggerating. It's only been six months since this new variant of the European rodent virus hit," a man in his early twenties said. "And the world pretty much had two healthy plague free years before that.

"Still feels like a century," Gerald insisted.

"What… ever," the teenage girl who joined the conversation piped up. "I just hope some townies come and join us."

"Well, it is Halloween and we are having a party in the only place that has enough space to socially distance," the young man pointed out.

There were at least two hours of daylight left but Gerald looked up at the pale round disk of the daytime moon. "Wow, another full moon this month and on Halloween too."

Misty, who'd been home from college since this particular pandemic closed her school, smiled, her white teeth gleaming in the sunshine. "Finally, a blue moon. Tonight will definitely be a twice in a full moon."

Everyone in their campground had been overjoyed when Misty had come home and suggested the Socially-Distant-Can't-Come-Without-A-Mask Halloween bash for the surrounding communities. Living far away from their RV commune next to the cemetery had definitely made Misty think outside their box.

By the time the sun hit the treetops the food was out, the drinks and bowls of sweets were set up on the flat tops of tombstones and Gerald cranked the music up. The sun sank lower in the sky and the gravestones threw long shadows all around the grass dance circle. The small mobile community of 15 families waited.

And waited.

The commune leader, Elliot, sighed. "Looks like a dud. A huge disappointment. We all really needed this exercise in community with the town folk."

Misty, heading for the dance circle, yelled, "The hell with it! Let's dance until it's time."

Elliot nodded, "Yes, let's party. Gerald, put on some good, old-fashioned disco."

131

The music got louder and faster and the first car pulled up. Then a second. Then a dozen more. People tentatively got out and approached the commune members. "Uh, thanks for holding this shindig," the woman from the first car said while keeping her distance.

"Our pleasure," Elliot said back. "Come, let's enjoy a beautiful evening and get to know each other better."

The woman nodded and watched her three children run to a table laden with bowls of orange and yellow candy corn. Gerald's eyes followed the oldest girl who had just jumped out of the car. He stood nearby and nervously cleared his throat. "Um… uh… hi?" he half said, half asked. "I'm, uh, Gerald."

"Hi," she said back. "Allison. How come I've never seen you in school?"

"Well, I'm home schooled. Everyone here is homeschooled. We, uh… move a lot."

"Must be cool," Allison said, giggling. "No homework, or is it all homework? Anyway," she said turning and bouncing her long, curly hair which was swept up in high ponytail, "Gerald, like my costume?" She laughed and twirled around to show off her poodle skirt.

Gerald swallowed and nodded, although his eyes were focused on her tight little angora sweater.

"What are you?" Allison asked.

Gerald brushed back his thick, black hair and touched his leather jacket, "The teenage werewolf."

"Cool," she said. "We're from the same movie. Let's take a walk."

The sun was down totally below the treetops as Gerald and Allison strolled between the dead and buried. "Really creepy place for a party." Allison giggled again. "Great idea."

Gerald listened to the sounds coming from the party hidden somewhere out of their line of sight. "Yes, a great idea."

Then he leaned over and kissed her.

She responded and before he knew it, they were groping each other between the tombstones. He couldn't believe his luck. He could guess she was popular, probably a cheer leader and yet here she was on the ground with him. He kissed her again and was reaching under her sweater when he heard the screams. She pushed him off and gasped. "What's that?"

He wanted to give the rehearsed answer, "Oh just a video," but he didn't. He wanted her in the best way and he sighed, because in a few minutes he'd have her in much worse way.

"Allison, the moon is rising."

She stared at him with wide eyes, her lips trembling.

"Allison, my family, our... our community are werewolves. Blue-Moon werewolves. We. . . we only get to hunt during the second full moon of a month."

The moon glow lit the area around them.

He grimaced and continued. "We hunt and humans die. It's just the way it is. Some years we hunt twice and sometimes we go a couple of years between blue moons. But now, we are hungry and

133

we like the cemeteries, makes the hunt more fun. So... so Allison, Allison, you gotta run."

Allison sat frozen until the moonbeam hit Gerald directly and then she screamed jumped up and ran between the grave markers.

Gerald watched her retreat, threw his head back and howled with regret as his hormonal teenage lust turned to feral blood lust instead. Then he shifted onto all fours and went to have her in the worst way.

He knew that in the early hours of morning, as the predawn moon set, everyone in their community would clean up, pull up roots and find another cemetery far away, maybe on another continent this time.

An unknown place to set up home for a while.

At least until the next blue moon.

# A Graveyard Haunting
## Stuart Holland

It began as a teenage prank, but it ended up as something much more sinister.

The graveyard of St. Nicholas The Fearless had always been a public thoroughfare. The church itself was disused and had fallen into disrepair. Several generations had passed since the last vicar, a woman by the name of Clarissa Thrush, had died suddenly at the age of forty seven. On 31$^{st}$ October she had been locking the church doors and felt the first pangs of the impending heart attack. Her corpse had been found the following morning on the church steps by an early dog walker. Since that fateful day, no services had taken place in the church and the graveyard, long since in decline, had fallen into sad state of neglect. Or at least it had been until the local Council had erected bench seating around the two great Yew trees that grew on either side of the footpath roughly halfway down the graveyard from the church.

It was this particular 31$^{st}$ October three teenagers, Mike, Peter and Andy, decided they would test the local folklore for themselves. It was said, if the night of 31$^{st}$ October fell on a Friday, if you sat under the Yew tree to the left of the path an hour before midnight you would hear a rustling in the tree, followed by a loud groan and then the ghost of Clarissa Thrush would come down from the tree, enter the door of the church and disappear.

"Okay, so it sounds daft," said Peter as the three of them sat round his computer, having searched the local archives for the details of this piece of folklore.

"It would be, but there are records going back to just a few years after she died that show several people witnessed the same thing," Andy responded.

"Well, today's Friday 31$^{st}$, so anyone up for a bit of a lark? We could just say we're going to a youth event, parents won't think we're up to anything."

"Okay, I guess," Mike was always the most reticent of the group. "The worst that can happen is we wait there until midnight and - nothing."

A few hours later, the three teenagers said goodbye to their respective parents and went out as if to a youth event, at around eight in the evening. Being teenagers with bottomless stomachs, they visited a local takeaway shop and hung around town until ten thirty before making their way to the graveyard. The derelict church and surrounding area were quiet and, as forecast, light rain was falling. Streetlights at either end of the pathway gave an almost eerie and foreboding light. The air was chill and a light breeze made it feel even colder. The three lads were dressed for the weather - a little rain was not going to stop them and at sixteen they most definitely didn't want to be stuck indoors. They passed the church building and the wrought iron door with the name of the church above it.

"I wonder who St. Nicholas the Fearless was?" Andy was one step ahead of the others.

"We can check it out tomorrow. Now, which Yew tree is in the folklore?"

The two trees were about fifty yards ahead of them, marking the midpoint of the pathway.

"Left," said Mike sombrely.

The teenagers went and sat on the wooden bench surrounding the tree.

"Ten to eleven," noted Andy. "I told my Mum I'd be back before midnight."

"We'll be back well before then. If this folklore turns out to be what I suspect it is, rubbish, then we'll be gone in fifteen minutes which might be just as well. this rain is starting to get heavier.

The minutes ticked by relentlessly. Then, in the distance they heard the town clock chime the hour.

"So, it's eleven. Anyone see anything?"

The voice wasn't Andy's, Mike's Peter's, but it was similar to all of them.

"Shiiit, who said that?" The boys had all been looking at each other when the voice came. They swung round, wildly looking for the source of the words. Nothing. They looked at each other, scared. That was when the leaves in the Yew tree rustled.

"Okay, this is scary," said Mike who looked like he wanted out of there.

"It's just a bit of wind in the tree," Peter responded, always the bravest of the three of them.

"I don't like it," Mike continued. "Too much like the story."

At that moment something like a loud groan, high above their heads, filled the air. Then there was another sound as the great bough of the tree right over them cracked loudly. The three lads

137

barely had time to look up at what was happening, much less, time to escape from their impending doom.

"Nooooo!" Peter said with an air of finality as the bough of the tree fell towards them. In the final seconds of their presence on earth, all three boys saw the same thing. The eerie sight of a figure dressed in black carrying what looked like a scythe and beside that figure, the old vicar in all her flowing robes falling through the tree, beckoning the boys to join her as she returned once more to the church she had served.

And in years to come, when the devastation of the night's events had begun to fade, a new folklore would come into being as Clarissa Thrush prepared for her next assault on the good people of the parish she had served.

138

# Legride and the Matter of the Ripper Murders
## Scott Harper

Stifling brown fog filled the cobbled streets of Whitechapel, diffusing the flickering yellow light of the ambient gas lamps and masking the radiance of a waxing gibbous moon. Few pedestrians were out this Samhain Night to celebrate the beginning of the darker half of the year, for terror had come to Whitechapel. Prostitutes had been murdered, their throats cut, organs removed, bodies discarded in alleyways with the trash. The police were baffled—no leads, no arrests, no suspects identified.

The press had given the fiend a name, an appropriate title for the terror he brought: Jack the Ripper.

Legride Kostaki, Bloodmaster of London, resolved to deal with this mortal who had caused such havoc in his borough.

He walked confidently through the deserted streets, refreshed from his daylight sleep. He wore black, a color suited to his personality and mood. A large cape billowed behind him in the evening breeze. Legride was well acquainted with the borough: Whitechapel, along with the rest of the East End, had been his private hunting grounds for over three hundred years from the time he defeated the prior Bloodmaster, an old Carpathian named Torgo, in a duel to the death. He still wore the deceased vampire's fangs on a necklace underneath his waistcoat and shirt as both a trophy and a reminder of the long path he'd traveled.

It was a privilege to have the run of such a normally-bustling borough, so near the heart of London herself. Whitechapel was in large part composed of a transient population, people coming and going at all hours, conducting all manner of personal and financial business. And while the main streets were well lit, the alleys were dark places where strange activities occurred—where lovers found freedom, thieves divvied up their loot and murderers dumped bodies.

Where a vampire might feed at length, undisturbed, Legride mused inwardly.

And Legride had fed here—copiously, wantonly, gluttonously—for over three centuries.

But now the terror had arrived in Whitechapel; Jack the Ripper had come to Whitechapel and the fiend's activities were threatening Legride's nightly feedings.

The sight of a boy in dirty, worn clothing selling newspapers on the corner caught the vampire's attention. He was struck by the young man's boldness, daring to venture out while many frightened adults hid inside their domiciles. The child's golden aura shined brightly in the night, a vessel of innocence.

"Get your paper here, read about the Ripper Murders!" the boy shouted.

Legride approached and looked him in the eye.

"Paper, guv'nor? Three pence," the boy said, offering Legride a daily with his grimy hand.

"What is your name, boy?" Legride inquired as he accepted the paper, reaching into his coat pocket.

"William, sir," the boy replied.

Legride removed a gold sovereign and flipped the coin into the air with his thumb. The boy caught it and looked at the shiny object with wide incredulous eyes.

"A sovereign!" he marveled. "Thank you, sir!"

Legride did not return the boy's enthusiasm—courtesy was his strong suit. "These streets are no place for you to be tonight, William," he admonished. He leaned forward, his ink-black hair framing the sharp, asymmetrical lines of his features. "There are monsters afoot. So best beat feet and run home. Hug your parents, for you know not when odd circumstance will snuff out their short lives."

William looked dismayed as Legride walked by him and then stopped to read the paper.

The front-page article did not please the vampire. The previous night the police had discovered another butchered female corpse, bringing the total of Ripper murders to five.

No doubt there are others, bodies the police have yet to discover, the vampire mused.

He looked around to see if there was anyone nearby watching him. When he was satisfied he was unobserved, he darted into an alley.

Unknown to Legride, William had followed him. The boy watched in awe as his most recent customer rose effortlessly off the ground and disappeared into the night sky.

141

The vampire hovered hundreds of feet above Devonshire Street, his supernaturally keen senses penetrating the night and the fog, probing for anything out of the ordinary. The red thirst was upon him, setting his body aflame with the need to feed.

Over many centuries of trial and error, Legride had found that the Undead needed to feed at least every other night, to claim a victim before daybreak to fuel their supernatural abilities. Strength, speed, near invulnerability—these legendary powers came with a price. The fresh blood from a kill renewed not only the physical body but also the mind and spirit. The psychic flood released at the moment of the victim's death nurtured the vampire brain, giving it the ability to shrug off the grim torpor of death each night when it rose from its coffin.

The Ripper had robbed Legride of his usual victims. The women of the night, the streetwalkers that frequented Whitechapel, had provided the vampire with ample sustenance and little threat of exposure. Their disappearances drew scant attention in a borough with a population always in flux. The shortage of prey greatly affected Legride; he felt his great strength beginning to wane. With no warm blood, the red thirst had become all-consuming, his body filled with a creeping cold premonition of final death. The vampire feared that he might act recklessly in his weakened condition, leading to his discovery. And while he possessed the strength of twenty men, he knew his most significant power was the general populace's lack of belief in his kind. Should the existence of the Undead ever graduate to more than whispered legends and gory stories in the penny dreadfuls, the age of the Bloodmasters would come to an abrupt, stake-filled end.

Legride's instincts told him the fiend would strike again tonight, that the man was consumed with bloodlust and could not stop himself. The attacks had been building, both in frequency and savageness, as Samhain had approached. He vampire was a supernatural creature itself self and could feel the barriers between worlds gradually easing, the light merging into the dark. And tonight, more than any time of the year, the living would be prey to the unnatural beings—whether ghost, fairy, or pooka—loosed upon the world.

He scoured the night in search of prey, Legride recalled the Samhain Night a millennia ago when he had been inducted into the ranks of the Undead. He'd been just a young sorcerer then, obsessed with unlocking the hidden secrets of the universe. To that end, he'd traveled to Ireland from his native Scotland and set up in an abandoned graveyard, preparing a divination ritual. That night, as the land hovered between the light of summer and the dark of winter, he lit a bonfire and ringed it with stones. He had waylaid a pale, scarlet-tressed young woman in a nearby town and tied her to a stone tomb perfectly aligned to greet the sunrise. Legride had discerned through his contacts that the girl was the first-born of seven children in her family, her genealogy making her a potent source of eldritch power to fuel his ritual. He methodically cut her body with a ceremonial dagger engraved with ancient Babylonian characters, whispering guttural incantations in a long-forgotten tongue and beseeching the arrival of a Fomorian demon with otherworldly knowledge to bestow upon him.

However, it was not a demon that responded to his offering. Legride felt the temperature plunge as a shadowy form resolved itself from the night. It latched long fang teeth to the maiden's throat and gorged itself on her blood. When it was full and bloated like a great leech, the creature beckoned him with a long-nailed hand, its vermillion eyes blazing in the dark. It offered knowledge of a kind, as well as strength and eternal life. Legride allowed himself to be drawn into that black embrace, felt the coldness of the fangs as they dug deep into his neck. He fell into darkness.

He dug his way out of a shallow grave the next night, his strong hands bursting through the loose earth as he rose in a grim parody of birth. His killer stood above him, silhouetted by the full moon. The creature spoke to him as its grave shroud flapped in the gusty wind, a whisper that grated inside his skull, harsh as tree bark.

"Mark always the anniversary of your turning on the Samhain. The realm of the dead calls out to our kind on such nights, seeking to reclaim those who have cheated its cold embrace."

Legride recalled the ancient vampire's words as a woman's shriek drew his attention. He shot higher into the sky and flew over the brick buildings, then hovered over a dark alley branching off Goulston Street, near Spitalfields Market. His keen night eyes penetrated the shadows.

He saw a blonde streetwalker, wearing a blue overskirt and black boots, struggle frantically with a shadow come to life. The vampire dropped out of the gray night sky as gently as a falling leaf, settling behind the combatants. He noted the shadow was a tall man dressed in black clothing, sporting a black cape and billycock hat. The dark man forced a white cloth over the woman's mouth with gloved hands. Legride's sensitive nose detected the pungent odor of chloroform.

The vampire recalled the press accounts of the previous Ripper murders. Scotland Yard detectives had concluded that The Ripper was drugging his victims before cutting their throats and disemboweling them. Legride's spirit soared—his search was over.

The vampire stepped forward and placed a vise grip on The Ripper's shoulder, preparing to turn him around. Legride was taken aback when the man twisted in his grasp. The cape tore under the force of the vampire's supernatural strength. The dark man retaliated and smashed a bottle of liquid chloroform on Legride's head. The power of the blow, coupled with the shock of inhaling such a large amount of liquid anesthetic, would have felled a normal man but Legride had been neither normal nor a man for over ten centuries.

The young streetwalker used the distraction to run out of the alley toward the street light's sanctuary. Legride ignored her as he wrapped his fingers around The Ripper's neck with serpentine speed. He felt the man's breath catch in his throat as the windpipe shut off. Then, exerting just a fraction of his great strength, Legride lifted his opponent into the air and tossed him fifty feet further back into the alley. The man landed hard, smashing through abandoned wooden crates and rolling over several times before coming to rest.

Legride walked confidently to his fallen foe, savoring his apparent victory. He felt invigorated, the eldritch energies that fueled his existence were more potent on Samhain Night than any other night of the year. The winds of magic buoyed both his strength and spirit. Though he seldom fed from male victims, their blood marred by the acrid taste of bitter hormones, he was willing to make an exception in this case for the man who had caused him so much hardship and deprivation. The vampire rubbed his hands together feverishly in anticipation, his long nails scraping against themselves as his snake-like tongue slipped out over his lips.

Legride grabbed the Ripper by the shoulder and flipped him over. The man sat up and suddenly jabbed a surgeon's scalpel deep into Legride's Undead heart, catching the vampire off guard. Legride reared but then righted himself. He looked down at the blade sticking out of his sternum and laughed.

"Common metal cannot harm me, cur!" he snarled with contempt, backhanding his assailant and sending him careening off a nearby wall.

Legride had been shot and stabbed with all manner of metal weapons over the centuries. Such injuries caused him no more discomfort than would a passing breeze. Only weapons made of organic material, either wood or bone that had once been part of a living (if not sentient) creature, were capable of delivering lasting damage to his kind.

He tried to remove the scalpel when sudden pain shot through him, causing him to stagger. Legride's hands burned instantly on contact with the blade. His vision swam as the Ripper rose to his feet.

Legride's blow had broken the dark man's neck; the vampire had heard the bones shatter under the force of his supernaturally strong impact. Yet somehow, the fiend still stood, his head lolling at an unnatural angle. Legride watched in disbelief as the man placed a hand on each side of his face and tugged, jerking the head back into position with an audible CRACK!

The dark man brushed off his clothing as he sauntered over to Legride, immobilized. The vampire could see now that the man was Caucasian, tall and pale with a slim mustache. Madness gleamed in hollow black eyes that rested far back in the skull. Wickedness beamed in his wide-faced, crooked-toothed grin. Unlike the golden innocence of the newspaper boy, the Ripper's aura was black and roily. Legride wondered what type of evil possessed a man who could recover so quickly from the vampire's attack.

The Ripper spoke in a resonant, condescending voice wedded to a cockney accent. "I see it in your red eyes, boss, the pain, the awe. The shock. You're wonderin' who ol' Saucy Jack is, no doubt? Why

147

he's chasin' all your girls away? How he brought you to your knees on the Samhain when your powers are at their peak? Well, Bloodmaster Kostaki, I'm Jack the Ripper, and I'm from Hell, sir!"

The Ripper surged forward, grabbing the scalpel. In a brutal economy of movement, he pulled it from Legride's chest and slit the vampire's throat from ear to ear. Raw pain erupted from the wound as Legride's black ichor sluggishly oozed out. The vampire attempted to heal his injuries, but the tear began to smoke. He lost his balance and fell on his back, his frantic red eyes darting from side to side in his head.

"Blessed metal, that's wot it is," the Ripper added. Light reflected off the mother-of-pearl buttons on his patented leather boots. He slowly walked over and looked down into Legride's agonized face.

"Helped meeself to a few crucifixes from Saint Mary's, I did, right in the middle of the night when no one was lookin', all them soddin' clergymen asleep. Melted them down, nice and proper, then coated me work tools with them. They're still wicked sharp, as you can tell."

Legride gurgled an incomprehensible curse in response, his fangs shredding his lips.

The Ripper's eyes blazed with cold insanity. "Ahhh, you're upset with me, no doubt. Can't see as I blame you—ol' Jack took away your power. But you see, Legride, ol' Saucy Jack has had his eyes on you for a while. Seen you come saunterin' 'round me borough like you owned the place, all high and mighty and full of yourself. Seen you help yourself to me women, Jack's whores, and use 'em up. Eat 'em up, literally. But they're mine, you see; Jack's whores. And you're interfering with me work, more than any lot of peelers ever have.

The Ripper continued speaking as Legride squirmed on the ground. "Found me calling in the organ trade, I did. Bit of a ghoul, some might say, a high-grade resurrectionist. Slice the throat, harvest a uterus or a heart or a liver, grand work and lots of good money in it. These London pagans will pay any price for special ingredients for their rituals and spells. They get all worked up Samhain Night, assertin' they can speak with spirits and bind demons to their will, would you believe? Now, imagine how much more these same sods are goin' to be willin' to come up with for a nice, live vampire, such as yourself, to spice up their Samhain sacrifice?" The Ripper's grin widened even further. "Well, I suppose 'live' isn't the proper term in your case now, is it?"

Legride tried to stand, but found all his strength had departed with his blood. He couldn't die, at least not in this manner. There was a prescribed ritual for vampire destruction: First, a stake would need to transfix his head, then his head severed before the body could be burned and the ashes scattered in running water, releasing whatever remained of his soul. But the wounds inflicted by the Ripper's scalpel had left him completely helpless. He focused his energy one last time. On countless prior occasions, he had reached out his will and tried to seize a mortal mind. His eyes

149

blazed crimson in the alley darkness as he touched the fiend's turbid psyche and commanded him to stop. Legride's efforts proved fruitless. The cold blue eyes that looked down on him beamed with appalling lunacy he could not impede, let alone control.

The Ripper shrugged off Legride's attempt at compelling him and proceeded with his pompous rant. "Oh, and Jack's got books, don't you know? Done lots of readin' in me time. Studied up on the legends of your sort—your strengths, flaws, what can hurt you, what can't, etcetera, etcetera. I made time to talk with a necromancer or two. They knew your name. Guess you've managed to make yourself a fair share of enemies over the years, Legride me chum. Found out your lot is pretty much almighty after sunset, especially on a night like tonight. But the books all concurred that holy trinkets worked wonders on you lot—robbed you of all your weird powers. I just had to come up with me own special way to use 'em." The Ripper held the bloody scalpel in front of him as the fog overhead parted, allowing the moonlight to shine off the keen metal.

Legride's vision darkened. It occurred to him that he had merely played at being evil, only dabbled in it. True, he had witnessed wickedness in various forms over the centuries. His creator had seemed the very personification of the term and Legride had sought to imitate him in many ways. He had pursued a chaotic form of evil and enjoyed the casual cruelty of toying with his victims, the game of cat and mouse, the look of terror and awe

150

and lust in their eyes as he claimed them. The outcome had never been in doubt. He had lived hot-tempered and vicious, arbitrarily violent and unpredictable.

But this dark man was different and had a much dissimilar stench of evil about him. There was an order, almost a lawfulness, to the malevolence he represented—a methodical devotion to inflicting the maximum amount of humiliation and destruction of other beings. Legride and his petty intrigues, his low-level chaotic maliciousness, meant small pickings in the overall hierarchy of evil. And now he lay overwhelmed and shattered on the ground of an abandoned alley, feeling like a small child in comparison to the magnificent malignancy that was Jack the Ripper. Legride wondered what hellhole the evil that possessed the fiend had come from.

"Now ol' Saucy Jack figures you want to know what's coming next, eh, Legride? Well, I won't make you walk three times around a grave to find out like these pagans would have you do. I'll tell you your future right now. You've been around these parts for such a long time and you've got lots of presents to give—blood and bone and fang and heart and brain. I'll fetch a proper sum for your parts. You're of sturdy stock, no doubt; I'm sure it will be a long, long time before you give up the ghost and go all dusty on me."

The Ripper bent down and began to slice agonizingly through his sternum. Legride lamented the fact that even a master vampire couldn't scream through a severed throat.

# Vengeful Spirits
## Olivia Arieti

The spirits were annoyed. Every year at Halloween, strangers kept knocking on their door and some went as far as entering the house. The structure, now abandoned, looked haunted and attracted all those on the lookout for chilling thrills on such a night.

Many were the rumours about it, locals swore to have seen more than a ghost roaming in there. For sure, the owners, Harry and Betty, were among them; the wealthy young couple, who had been brutally murdered, were said to have stepped out of their graves and gone back there to wait for their killer, confident that he would return to search for the money and jewels he hadn't been able to find.

Their moans and howls didn't intimidate the dauntless intruders but soon the spectres became the objects of derision.

"Come out, you stupid ghosts, show us that you really exist," the tomboys would cry, while others sneered, "We have treats for you," and showers of eggs against the broken panes followed.

The situation worsened when the place became the refuge of the homeless and derelict souls in search of shelter. They would remain a few nights, careless of their presence, before setting forth again on their endless wanderings.

Unable to bear the ongoing disturbance of their privacy, the phantoms promised to make that

Halloween the last time a mortal would trespass the threshold.

The wind was wailing and menacing clouds had already billowed up the sky; ghastly shadows dwelled in the dying light and the atmosphere was as bleak and gloomy as required by the occasion.

Bruce was exhausted. He had been wandering around for days, unable to find a bed, not even in the House of the Poor. It had been unusually cold that week and his roaming made him already feel like one of the spirits about to populate the evening.

Although familiar with the decrepit house and its stories, he pushed the rickety door open. His hands were turning blue and his face was too stiff to imagine spending the night outdoors.

He had just entered and was settling his sleeping bag near the disused fireplace, probably with the illusion that the soot and ashes still treasured some warmth, when Harry appeared before him with the intent to scare the bloke out of his skin.

"This is your big chance, young man," he said, while dealing the cards, "no more misery for you if you beat me."

Bruce gazed at him and, without a word, got hold of the cards and started playing.

After a short while, the ghost shouted triumphantly, "Got to pay me now or you'll be my guest forever, you fool!"

Even if reluctant, the poor fellow had to admit he was before a supernatural creature.

"Wait, Spectre," he shouted, "I can pay you more than the amount I've just lost... I'll tell you who murdered you and your wife."

"Speak up," cried Betty who plummeted into the room.

"Who's the asshole?" thundered her husband.

Bruce closed his eyes for a second with the hope that the dreary figures might disappear but on opening them again, he saw they both stood before him, more enraged than ever.

He revealed how he'd been sleeping in a recess under the town's main bridge with a guy called Joe, who kept boasting about his criminal deeds. The murder of that house's owners ranked among them. Then the heinous fellow said he would celebrate Halloween by going back and finally get hold of the riches he had to leave behind.

At once, the ghosts vanished as though eager to prepare an infernal plan for their imminent guest.

Bruce looked around. What was going on there? Had he fallen asleep and was living a nightmare? Had he really played cards with a spectre of perhaps, someone who had frozen to death and was already in the other world? The only thing he was sure of was the criminal's promise.

By now twilight had withdrawn, leaving the total dominium to her dark successor. Drafts had made their way through the broken shutters and the room was cold and grim.

He was still pondering the event when Lily entered.

154

"The weather's too nasty to wait for my clients on the street. They seem to have more fun knocking on stupid doors than making love."

"I believe this is not the right place to for you, doll, not tonight at least."

The harlot gazed at him, "Hey, I know you! You're the one who saved me from that maniac's grasp. He would have killed me if it hadn't been for you."

Bruce was about to reply when she moved close and smiled alluringly, "I owe you a favour, man."

He gazed at Lily. Her smile was inviting and the Miss Dracula costume very seductive... What if those spectres didn't exist at all and were simply a deadly trick of his weary mind and body? The place, even if most scary, would be all theirs...

"Wouldn't mind paying you back tonight, sweetie."

"What is it, baby," he muttered, "a special treat?"

"Consider it so, I'm sure you'll love being bitten, hon. Besides, I need to be warmed up, almost froze in this stupid costume."

"I'll take care of that," he whispered by now totally kindled by the girl's wantonness.

He was about to untie the corset when Joe burst in, wild and furious.

He recognised Bruce. "So you're a spy, huh? Bet you've come to warn those damned spooks. Tonight's their night and you know it, bloody bastard!"

He hadn't finished talking but the killer took out his knife and plunged it into the guy's body.

"So you're the lousy creep," shouted Harry who had stormed in with his companion.

"Nice to see you again, guys," sneered Joe as he got hold of Lily and pointed the blade at her throat.

"Needless to say she'll end up like you if you dare to move closer."

Lily was as terrified as bewildered. She was unable to understand what was going on and kept moving her eyes from the spirits to the corpse, from the corpse to her potential assassin, unable to cry or shout.

Now the tormented shadows were hovering to and fro, fuelled by fierce revenge; although aware that they could tighten their clammy hands around the villain's neck, they wanted to spare the poor girl, she was too young to join them.

An unexpected leap of Bruce's spirit startled all the bystanders, mortal or not; his hollow howl made the man vacillate and in the wink of an eye the knife was snatched and dug into the criminal flesh.

"Just like you did with me, bastard."

"Glad to have you with us," smiled Betty and stretched out her skeletal hand, thankful for his deed.

Although Bruce's features had turned rigid, they showed all the distress of ranking among his ghastly companions.

Only then Lily seemed to realise what had happened and moved close to her saviour. She caressed his face tenderly and uttered, "Thank you once again, dear, I'll miss you."

Then she kissed the stiffened lips that unexpectedly curled into a wistful smile.

Immediately after, she ran out and, in tears, tried to explain what happened to two officers who were patrolling the streets. Although she urged them to go into the house, which she kept addressing as inhabited by terrifying uncanny creatures, her narration was so confusing and unreal, that they hurriedly dismissed her, certain that it was nothing but a silly Halloween trick.

On noticing the stains of blood on her costume while undressing, Lily had the proof that it hadn't been a nightmare but a real murder tinged with ghastly horror. The following morning she would bring the garment to the police and prove she was telling the truth.

The girl couldn't know that the spirits had removed the murderer's corpse and now were feasting their revenge and their spectral guest's arrival.

To avoid further disturbances and visits, before the crack of dawn they had also wiped away the stains from the girl's dress that now hung as good as new for the following Halloween.

# All Hallow's Eve
## Rie Sheridan Rose

When the witch winds howl
on All Hallow's Eve,
the Wiccan take back their
sacred night.

They shut their doors to
sugar-rushing children
and gather instead
in kinship rite.

Rituals passed down through time
circle around their band,
reaffirming what is theirs,
in Nature's sight.

Blood calls to blood as charms
are laid to heal or harm
as befits the recipient…
Black magic intertwines with light.

The wards are laid to protect their kin,
and guard the dwellings they hold dear.
Old spells, fresh spells, spells for good,
and spells that blight.

In tireless circle, round they pace,
and gather strength from camaraderie.
Free to be themselves at last,
to loosen reins held tight.

When at last the candles burn out,
and chants fall away to chats,
they separate—renewed—
their auras bright.

To separate houses, lives, and dreams
the Wiccan go without complaint,
knowing that this night was theirs—
a brief delight.

# Halloween Again
## Wondra Vanian

Halloween. *Again.*

God, Morgan hated Halloween. It was nothing but an excuse for the city's youths to act like the little shits everyone but their parents knew they were.

The doorbell rang.

"Trick or treat!"

He groaned and turned up the volume on the television. More little bastards demanding their yearly tithe. Morgan ignored them. They rang the bell again. And again.

"Open up, jerkwad!"

"Yeah, we know you're in there!"

Ding-dong! Ding-dong! Ding-dong!

"That's it!"

Morgan pushed himself out of his recliner angrily, aging bones protesting the sudden movement, and stomped to the door. A can of pepper spray sat on the table by the door for occasions just like this. He grabbed it and held it out in front of him as he opened the door with a "Get out of here before I…"

The words died in his throat. There, on his doorstep, was a toddler in a black robe holding a plastic scythe a whole foot taller than he was. The toddler held out an orange, plastic bucket in the shape of a grinning jack-o-lantern.

"Twick or tweat."

Morgan looked around for the kids who'd been hurling abuse at him. Nothing. He looked for the toddler's parents. The kid couldn't have reached the doorbell on his own yet...

There was no one else around.

The child spoke again in a small, squeaky voice.

"Twick or tweat?"

"Uh, yeah. Sure, kid." Morgan tossed the small white and red can back onto the table. As much as he hated Halloween (children and other people in general) even he didn't have the heart to spray a three-year-old. But he didn't have any candy, either. "Just a sec."

He hurried to the kitchen, rooting around until he finally found a candy bar stuffed away in a drawer. It was a little beat up, but it was better than nothing. He grabbed the sad-looking bar and hurried back to the door...

Only to find his doorstep empty.

A noise behind him made Morgan turn. He wondered what kind of parents taught their kids that it was okay to walk into someone's house uninvited. No wonder little brats these days had so few manners; it all came down to the parents. Scum raised scum.

Annoyance filled Morgan's voice as he said, "Here you go..." Holding out the battered chocolate bar, he looked down at the toddler.

Except... it wasn't a toddler.

A grown man stood behind Morgan, towering his crooked frame by several inches. The man was dressed in Death's black robes and held a gleaming

161

scythe that stood a whole foot over his head. There was no flesh on the man's face, only white bone.

"Tank oou," Death said in that same small, squeaky, childlike voice. How could... it sounded just like that kid... but...

Morgan opened his mouth—to say *what*, he didn't know—but nothing came out. The chocolate bar fell to the floor. His lifeless body soon followed.

When the group of rowdy teenagers returned later that evening with several boxes of eggs, they found the cranky old man's door wide open. One found the courage (with the help of a little goading from his friends) to walk up and poke his head inside. What he saw there made him fear Halloween for the rest of his life.

He dropped the box of eggs he held by the body and ran, the expression of terror on his face a mirror image of the old man's.

# Whispering Wood
## Wendy Lynn Newton

Tommy Hadfield's one to talk.

Scrumpin' through Pitcher's farm and leaving a trail of broken corn behind him, all snapped shafts and scattered heads and trampled ground, like some random, half-assed crop-circle he didn't put enough thought into designin' right. On his way to Badger Creek, he says, so I go, you know, "I'm comin' too." There's me, runnin' behind him like a stray dog tryin' to catch up, yappin' at him to wait up and feelin' the sweat rolling down my back 'cause it's the hottest day yet, but he's off, straight through the crop and headin' sideways for Whispering Wood.

I says, "Don't go there!" but Tommy's not one to listen.

If you heard anything about Haddie it's that he don't hear from one ear to the goddamn next a thing you say to him, 'less he wants to. And that's only when there's summin' in it for him.

You heard the time he tipped the cows in Yabbie's field? Stinkin' drunk from the bottle of shine his Gramps makes and hollerin' for Cassie to come out and kiss 'em, cussin' at the top of his lungs when she don't and Yabbie took to the window with his 12 gauge. There Yabbie was, nuthin' but a black outline against the glass with the kitchen light spillin' out behind him 'cause his missus has gone to bed, right, that 12 gauge cocked and aimed right at Haddie, but Haddie doesn't blink an eye. One minute he's spittin' on the dirt and tellin' Yabbie it's one way or the other and she's gonna choose him, next he's skirtin' and weavin' like a rabbit chased by a fox under a full moon as Yabbie's shot pings at the dirt 'round his feet. Doesn't stop Haddie havin' the last shot, though.

That's the other thing about Tommy Hadfield.

He likes havin' the last word.

So he's like, "I'm going in, you coming too? Or you gonna let that talk you heard about it chicken you out, like the Momma's boy they says you are?"

Then he starts clucking and buck-buck-bucking and flappin' his arms and struttin' like he's peckin' that corn from the floor of the hay barn and what was I to say?

All I seen was the bottoms of his new pussy-white sneakers and the black dirt rufflin' behind 'em as they flew into that corn field and he's headed for the Woods. Them broken cornstalks stickin' and scratchin' in places I'm tellin' you that you don't wanna be stuck and the air 'strictin' in my lungs from the crush of the corn and the 'xertion of tryin' to keep up and me sweatin' like a pig in Old Barney's smoker, wishin' I was anywhere right now but following Tommy Hadfield into Whispering Wood. But it's All Hallows, I don't wanna be left out.

He was gone right in before I catched him, the grey of his sweater and the black of his soles sucked right up like he was a ghost swallowed whole by that dark, dank place. I says, "Where you at, Haddie?" but he don't answer, so's I stops a minute, tryin' to suck back the air into my lungs stole by the run and that crushin' corn field, and thinkin' what I do next. I won't lie, every bit o' me was screamin', "Don't go in there!" then I hears Haddie's voice in the back of my head and think of him laughin' the way he does that way, his head thrown back and his lips splitting the whole width of his face and the boys laughin' right along with him when they find out another fuckin' stupid pussy-ass thing I've done. And there's me tryin' to explain, but nuthin's comin' out of my mouth.

Alls I do is sit there at the bar with the boys beside me, right, sucking back my piss and tryin' not to look at any of their goddamn laughin' faces and wishing Pitcher's farm dirt would swallow me whole up.

And alls I can see is the colour red.

The red of the cloth as I stare at the bar, the red of Haddie's laughin' goddamn fuckin' prick of a face, the red of the slash that's dripping faster down my arms, the red of Momma's eyes when she finds out what I done again.

The last laugh.

That's the other thing Tommy Hadfield likes having.

So's I go, okay, what fuckin' choice do I got right now? And it was like this light goes on in the back of my head and I can feel it buzzing, as if my skull was a fridge door that had just opened and I'm the hungry one swingin' on the hinges. I takes one last look at Pitcher's field like a drowning man stares at the beach and I'm in.

You think a cornfield's the worst place to get lost in. You think about how you push your way ahead, your arms out like a zombie, how the silks trail against your skin, the stalks stick into the back of your neck, the way your shoulders prickle from broken cobs of corn as you brush past. You try to see your way forward, but all you sees is that corn, endless miles of it, there's a golden sky of it towering every way you look and you know if you closed your eyes and spun around, you'd be lost in that shit forever. You try to hold it together while the air's being sucked from your lungs, but your brain's screamin' RUN just run, any way, doesn't matter which, just get the goddamn fuck out of here NOW!

You try to run, but you trip and as that corn tumbles down like an avalanche of mummies on top of you, you scream like a girl and wet your pants. And when Tommy Hadfield comes back and finds you like that, all red face and sobbing eyes and pissed pants, you wish the goddamn cornfield would open up like a mouth and swallow you the fuck whole.

You think a cornfield's the worst place you can get lost in and then you find yourself following Tommy Hadfield into Whispering Wood.

They says the dead live there, the ones that died at another's hand, howlin' at the stars when the moon's full and the Halloween dead are abroad and shakin' their fists at the fates what dragged them there, all bloated and bloodied and cut up. They says they like nothin' more than draggin' another one down with them, the ones with guilt for hearts and ice for blood, the ones who got away with it.

That's what I heard. You don't want to be caught on the wrong side of the moon in Whispering Wood. That's what Haddie told me that night I followed him into the cornfield and got lost, the night I pissed my pants and cut my wrists and made my mother cry.

But there Haddie runs now, his sneakers full of Pitcher's dirt, his hair stuck with cornstalks, his heart full of ice. Swallowed like a ghost.

I watch him slip into the dark and hold my breath, calling, "Tommy! Tommy! Where the fuck are you?" but the stillness swallows my voice and the dark eats at the soft part of my heart.

I go further in, right, until I can't sees my hand in front of my goddamn face. I don't know which way is right or left, which way's in or out, and I'm crying out, "Tommy! C'mon, you stupid-ass fuck-face, where the fuck are you?" but he don't answer.

I feel it then, creeping up behind me, the stinkin' breath on my neck of some filthy goddamn corpse, hear its bones rattlin' and crackin' as its rotten arms reach out to grab me, but I can't dare look. Then Haddie's behind me, screaming, "Boo!" and I feel the piss runnin' down my leg. And when he laughs like that, with his head thrown back and his lips splitting the whole width of his face, I see in my head all the boys laughin' right along with him when they find out another fuckin' stupid pussy-ass thing I've done.

And alls I can see is the colour red.

It's sprayin' the trees, it's drippin' down my arms from the branch I'm clutchin' tight in my fist, it's staining the cornstalks stuck in Tommy's hair.

167

The last place you want to get lost in is Whispering Wood. If only Haddie had thought to tell me that.

But that's another thing about Tommy Hadfield.

He doesn't think.

# 50% Halloween
## Dorothy Davies

It's not going so well this year, this Halloween thing. Something's missing, like – enthusiasm, determination, gore-covered outfits, freaky Goths, Haunted House signs and most of all, ghosts.

The problem is… there's a recession on even here in the night ether where ghosts, ghouls and bumpy things generally reside. I can't say 'live', that's misrepresentation and that brings Trading Standards people down on your head. Even here we are careful to be oh so correct in our interpretation of all that concerns our work of haunting, scaring, annoying and generally being a pest to the 'living'.

I mean, seriously, have you seen the ghost Trading Standards people? Bristling with pens, so they are, carrying clipboards wherein lie all the rules of the season of Samhaim: we can do this but we can't do that. We can go here but we can't go there. We can irritate but we cannot annoy. We can scare but we cannot terrify.

What's the point of Halloween if we can't terrify?

By the way, what's with the not leaving food and drink out any more for us passing spirits? Have you all forgotten the true nature of this night?

Obviously you have.

Then let me remind you.

Samhain is the end of summer and the start of winter. It is the night when souls are walking, unresting, seeking human companionship and all that might lead to in the way of death and destruction. To placate us and make sure we go right by and annoy/irritate/terrify (whoops, I meant scare, sorry...) someone else, you leave out food and drink for us.

It isn't there.

You're too busy trick-or-treat-ing and collecting bag loads of candy from householders who are too scared to risk 'trick'. We, the reason this festival exists, are forgotten. We are smothered under the need for jack o'lanterns, candy, apples, fancy dress and all.

Do you detect a touch of bitterness here?

Of course you do.

Wouldn't you be bitter if your one night of freedom, goodies and most of all, recognition, became a fun festival instead?

So I am appealing to those of you who understand the real true horror of Samhain, of Halloween, to come out in force and join us, in a manner of speaking, to put the whole thing back where it belongs, in the realm of darkness and spookiness and outright horror.

# When Your Skin
# is on the Pumpkin
## Dona Fox

I've seen Satan. You can run with him, even be his best friend and not know him for what he is for I believe that shinin' you on is part of his power, somethin' he never lost when he fell.

I was still innocent that last Halloween as Rudy and me ran down the sidewalk, me skipping over every crack, still believing I was somehow protectin' my mom.

I'd hollered and Rudy hadn't heard me, so I touched his arm. He was a coiled snake again, but that mood of his was gonna be more dangerous today. I couldn't let him take his fury out to the streets with all those innocent kids runnin' around alone. But I had to be careful; he was going to be extra touchy tonight. Not only was there a north wind, but like I said, it was Halloween.

Rudy was my best friend, so it fell on me to protect him from himself. And there was the matter of his backpack–it was so oddly misshapen.

"What's in there, man?" Ever the fool, I reached out once more. He twirled away–the wind tossed his hair into his eyes. He tripped on the flower border that lined Mrs. Bruskey's fence and fell onto his skinny ass.

"It's nothin'." He pushed at the dirt with the toe of his bright new Vans, then made a rough attempt to tap the flowers back into place. In the end all he did was leave a waffle-mark from the sole of his shoes, which was as good as a signature in the dirt. "Hurry 'fore Bruskey sees the mess and calls the cops-" his laugh was more like a bark "-let's go. It's just an empty box." The cold sun shot down between the trees and hit his face. His mouth formed a grim white line.

"What?" I tried to catch his glance.

Rudy looked square at me, "I picked up these skater shoes this morning," he winked and gave me his dang lopsided grin and I understood. He was wound tight 'cause he'd just stolen the shoes and hadn't ditched the box yet. I should have noted how hard his chin set right after the smile and how thin his skin stretched across the bones behind his face.

"You're not gonna tell on me, are you?" He stared at me and I realized how cold his gaze could be.

I felt goosebumps break out on my skin. "Of course not, Rudy. Never."

"Okay, then. Come on, let's hit the donut shop, then we'll see if the guys are at the shed already." Rudy gave me a pal-shove. I laughed, shoved him back and we trotted down the street side by side.

The old men were at their usual table–ashes in the bin, waiting for the wind to blow them away. I was sure they would sit outside the donut shop solving the problems of the universe, smoking and drinking coffee until they died.

I went in and Rudy stayed outside, staring at the old men, as he pretended to smoke the cigarette he always carried behind his ear.

Rudy would have left them alone even as they coughed, hacked up giant wads of phlegm onto the

172

cement and eyed us with scorn and contempt but for the fact one of them had a righteous dead-on aim.

Yep, one of those old codgers hacked up a wad of mucus from deep in his throat and a bit of greenish globule hit one of Rudy's new stolen Vans and rolled down the black and white checked material leaving a shiny trail like a slug.

I'd just come out the door, and I watched as it dangled off the toe of Rudy's new shoe.

Rudy said he'd not put up with that. He knew where these old codgers lived and tonight was Halloween. Then one of the plastic tables tipped over. The old men jumped up as hot coffee spilled everywhere. Maybe the table was about to go down already; maybe Rudy did it. I never saw what happened.

We ran.

The guys were already waiting at the clubhouse. It was an old shed we'd discovered in the woods behind my grandpa's place. There were four of us, friends since first grade, and Rudy. I couldn't quite remember when Rudy'd showed up, maybe last year or last week, but he fit in as if he'd been with us forever.

"We trick or treating tonight?" Mark held out brown paper grocery bags. His dad owned the local market, so we counted on him for our bags.

"Nah, we're too old. Last year was pushing it." I squelched the idea right away.

"I agree. It was embarrassing." Even Little Bruce was with me.

"Yeah, what old lady Bruskey said–I don't want to be talked to like that again, ruined the night for me, man." Jerry reached, took the bags from Mark.

"Okay, no treating then. What's left?" Mark let Jerry have the bags.

"TRICKS!" we cried out in unison, then we laughed at the warm feeling of being together, thinking alike.

"But what?" Mark was pouting over the loss of his bags and his last chance to be the guy we counted on.

"I have a plan," Rudy was really tall as he stood in the middle of the shed, "you know how those old guys like to spend so much time with their little pocket knives, seeing who can out-carve the other on their jack-off-o'-lanterns then they display them all lit up on their porches so the little kids will come beggin' for their candy? We used to play their games. No more."

"Yeah, Rudy?" He had my attention, but I was dubious.

Rudy jumped onto our only chair, looked down at us, and waved his arms as he talked. "Soon as it's dark, we'll start and we'll go on as long as it takes, past midnight, if we have to–and we'll rip every last pumpkin off all those old dudes' porches." Rudy's voice was hoarse.

"Yeah, man!" Mark pounded a fist in the air. "We can double up my bags and carry some of the smaller pumpkins in them."

"Good thinking, Mark! And we'll hide them all in Mrs. Bruskey's basement." Rudy grabbed the bags from Jerry and passed them out to the gang.

"What?" I couldn't believe his audacity.

"Yeah. Bruskey's basement door to the backyard is broken–it doesn't lock, doesn't even shut. Are ya with me!"

Of course we were.

We left, but Rudy hung back. I imagined he meant to plot something spectacular for our last Halloween.

\*\*\*

We'd been out all night when we finally met in front of Mrs. Bruskey's house. We were exhausted, but the fact it was Mrs. Bruskey's house and the last house on our list seemed to embolden us.

"Mrs. Bruskey!" I cooed, tapping a stick on her front gate, but light, half-hoping she wouldn't hear it.

"Trick or trick!" Mark waved a grocery bag above his head.

We climbed the fence and Little Bruce tip-toed up the vine-covered walkway. We followed him up the stone steps, across the porch and to the heavy front door.

"Are you in there?" Little Bruce whispered, his ear and his lips against the wood.

We all jumped when Jerry began to pound on the door, "Trick, trick, trick!" Then we took up the mantra and chanted with him, "Trick, trick, trick."

"She's hiding."

"She's not coming out."

"I saw Rudy talking to her yesterday; maybe he put her on notice to leave us alone."

"Yeah, Rudy probably put the fear in the old battle-axe."

"Where is Rudy?"

We ran to the huge windows on either side of the front door and realized no lights were on in the house.

"She's not home." I looked at the gang, hands and faces against the windows, mouths open, tongues pressed against the glass, drooling, "come on, guys, don't be crude. We're here for the pumpkins."

Mrs. Bruskey had plenty of jack-o'-lanterns displayed across her porch, candles burning to light the eyes and mouths, "gather them up and let's go around back to the basement door."

The back door was open a crack, just like Rudy said it would be.

Somebody found the light switch and everybody screamed.

Huge black flies were thick everywhere and blood was smeared across the whitewashed walls. An arm hung from the washing machine. Bowels were draped across the rafters like pink crepe paper at a baby shower. And the smell, how did Rudy manufacture a smell that could only come from a mixture of the foulest body fluids and a rotting corpse? That was just it; he couldn't have.

Though I figured Rudy had hung back to stage this blood and guts scene of horror just for us, something about it gave me maggots in my stomach–it was too real.

I was too weirded out to peek inside the washer but I had to and when I did Mrs. Bruskey stared back at me from the bottom of the machine, baby snakes raced from her mouth and a big, fat snake stared at me as it curled around her head. The snake's stare reminded me of Rudy, *You're not going to tell on me, are you?*

Rudy had gone too far.

I pushed the arm in and slammed the washer shut before the other guys could see. "Hey, Rudy, you got us good. Ha, ha, ha?" my voice echoed in the empty basement.

"So, where is Rudy?" Jerry's voice was trembling, "what do we do now? Do we leave the jack-o'-lanterns here?"

They all looked at me.

"No. Take as many as you can carry to our clubhouse," I said, perhaps foolishly, but then I wasn't used to being in charge.

We ran to the clubhouse with our stolen pumpkins, as if the devil was on our heels.

The inside of the clubhouse was dimly lit, thanks to several candles we'd set up earlier. It felt like a safe place in the middle of the dark forest on this, the scariest night of the year–our first night staying out this late–tricking, not treating.

Just as I was thinking how dangerous the night had become, several of the candles went out.

"This jack-o'-lantern feels funny. Oh, no. Here, touch this." Jerry thrust the pumpkin at Mark's belly.

177

"Oh, ick. You keep it." Mark tried to pass it back, "I dropped it, but look it rolled away–it's over there–"

Little Bruce peered around from behind me where he was tugging on my shirt, "What about it?" he squeaked.

"It's covered in skin," Mark backed away, "and it's crawling with little white worms."

"Maggots? And what do you mean...skin...?" I asked.

"Human?" Mark sounded like he was about to cry.

"Nah," I bent down but I saw it too, the pumpkin wrapped in skin with maggots crawling out of the eyes and darkness where the mouth should be, "where?" I asked anyway.

"In the pile, Mark just threw it down," Little Bruce dug his fingers into my arm.

"Are you sure it wasn't already there?" I asked as if it were a relevant question. But it seemed there were way more jack-o'-lanterns in our hideout than we could have carried in.

"Which house did this one come from?" Jerry turned to Mark.

"I dunno. Who dropped theirs in this corner?" Mark looked at Jerry, then Little Bruce and then me.

"Does it have a candle? Mine both had candles," Little Bruce came out from behind me.

I stepped closer and the blood leaking from the grinning mouth soaked my shoes. I saw movement inside the shell and, remembering the snakes in Mrs. Bruskey's washer, I jumped back.

"Where's Rudy? Who saw him last?" I looked at the guys they all shrugged and shook their heads; nobody'd seen him. "Okay, wait," I tipped the pumpkin with my toe and a giant blood-soaked rat scurried into the corner and disappeared.

"Rudy!" I called out, "that was epic! You can come out now," my laugh sounded false even to me. Would Rudy harm one of us–all of us? Now that I'd seen what he'd done to Mrs. Bruskey, was I danger?

Another dozen bloody jack-o'-lanterns rolled through the open door behind us, candles blazing inside.

"Rudy?" I called again, but not as loud. I didn't want him to answer. He wasn't in the shed. But we were cornered here. We could make a run for it. But was he waiting outside to grab us?

An old man's voice echoed through the woods and into our little hideout.

"When you're too old but you play with Halloween, anyway–it gets real, boys."

Twigs snapped in the woods outside. Big boots clomped through the underbrush unconcerned about what lay on the ground beneath them. The coughs and laughter of a dozen old men echoed through the woods as they stomped circles around our hide-out. Around and around, they chanted and stomped until daybreak.

During the night we smelled smoke as if the trees and brush were on fire, but we stayed huddled together in the shed. When we had enough light and courage to go out in the morning, the ground around our clubhouse was black, all the trees and

179

bushes had been burnt flat to the ground. Yet our shed stood untouched in the middle of a circle of gray ash.

We never saw hide nor hair of Rudy again.

I don't know if the same old men sat outside the donut shop after that or not. I believe it was the angle of the sun that prevented me from looking into their faces. But I got a faint scent of smoke off their boots when I walked by so I smiled toward them hoping it was thanks enough for their protection that Halloween night.

# Meet the Authors

**Diane Arrelle** has more than 350 short stories published and two short story collections: Just A Drop In The Cup and Seasons On The Dark Side. She, her sane husband and insane cat live on the edge of the New Jersey (USA) Pine Barrens (home of the Jersey Devil).

www.arrellewrites.com    FaceBook:    Diane Arrelle

**Olivia Arieti** lives in Torre del Lago Puccini, Italy, with her family. She writes drama, poetry and fiction. Her stories have appeared in several magazines and anthologies including, *Enchanted Conversations, Enchanted Tales Literary Magazine, Fantasia Divinity Magazine, Forgotten Tomb Press, Horrified Press, Infective Ink, Pandemonium Press, Sirens Call Publications, Blood Song Books, Black Hare Press, Pussy Magic Magazine, Stormy Island Publishing, Breaking Rules Publishing, Scarlet Leaf Review, Iron Faerie Publishing, Dark Dossier Magazine, Paramour Ink Press, Raven and Drake Publishing.*

**Dan Allen** is Canadian and enjoys spending time in Northern Ontario. You can find his short stories in numerous magazines, anthologies and podcasts. Visit www.danallenhorror.com to see a presentation of his published work.

His terrifying look at Alzheimer's, "Above the Ceiling," is featured in Bards and Sages collection of the Best Indie Speculative Fiction Vol. 2.

A personal favourite, "Sympathy for the Zingara," can be found in the March 2019 edition of ParAbnormal Magazine.

His terrifying story, "The Basement" (edited by Horror Zine's Jeani Rector), was published by Hellbound Books in July 2020.

You can visit Dan at www.danallenhorror.com and follow him on Facebook and Twitter at

@danallenhorror. You can write to Dan at contact@danallenhorror.com

**Dorothy Davies** is an editor, writer, photographer and medium. Somehow all these things come together in her seemingly crowded leisure and work life. She is an avid kindle user and delights in writing reviews for Amazon, especially when a novel is deleted a mere 2-3 chapters in and is too badly written to be read... she retired from editing for a while to run a second hand shop, the best one on the Isle of Wight, but the thrill of finding and publishing outstanding stories became too much so she started again with the Gravestone Press imprint. She still runs the shop...

**Michael H. Hanson** created the ongoing SHA'DAA shared-world anthology series currently consisting of "SHA'DAA: TALES OF THE APOCALYPSE", "SHA'DAA: LAST CALL", "SHA'DAA: PAWNS," "SHA'DAA:

FACETS", "SHA'DAA: INKED", "SHA'DAA: TOYS," and "SHA'DAA: ZOMBIE PARK", all published by Moondream Press (an imprint of Copper Dog Publishing). Michael's short story "C.H.A.D." appears in the Crystal Lake Publishing anthology "C.H.U.D. LIVES!", his short story "Rock and Road" appears in the Roger Zelazny tribute anthology "SHADOWS AND REFLECTIONS," and his short story "Born Of Dark Waters" appears in the Independent Legions Publishing anthology "THE BEAUTY OF DEATH 2: DEATH BY WATER." Michael also has stories in Janet Morris's Heroes in Hell (HIH) anthology volumes, "LAWYERS IN HELL," "ROGUES IN HELL," "DREAMERS IN HELL," "POETS IN HELL," "DOCTORS IN HELL," "PIRATES IN HELL," "LOVERS IN HELL," and "MYSTICS IN HELL." He has had over 100 short stories published in the fields of science fiction, fantasy, and horror, and he has written and published six collections of poetry: "AUTUMN BLUSH" and "JUBILANT WHISPERS" (Racket River Publishing), "DARK PARCHMENTS" and "WHEN THE NIGHT OWL SCREAMS" (MoonDream Press), and "ANDROID GIRL And Other Sentient Publications" and "QUARANTINE WORLD: Trapped in The Coronaverse" (Three Ravens Publishing).

**Scott Harper**: The world was just a tad dull and unimaginative for a young Scott Harper growing up in 1970's Southern California,. He found a creative outlet in the world of Marvel Comics, fervidly devouring the monthly adventures of Iron Man, Hulk, and Captain America. Later, his tastes turned toward the Marvel black and white magazines' more esoteric horror province, faithfully following titles such as *Dracula Lives*! and *Tales of the Zombie*. Influenced by these works and such great authors as Bram Stoker, John Steakley, and Marv Wolfman, Scott's unique writing style combines horror and fantasy elements with superhero-style action. When not writing, Scott spends his time either reading, working out at the gym, adding to his model collection, or walking his two dogs. He lives in California with his wife and son.

**Stuart Holland** is the owner of Fiction4All, a golf enthusiast (especially the 19th hole) and has written in the genres of crime/mystery, thrillers and suspense and has now turned his hand to horror. His books are available from fiction4all.com in both digital and print editions. His other interests include conspiracy theories, the Knights Templars and has a fascination for the paranormal and supernatural. Which may explain why he wrote 2020-Wipeout a couple of years before Covid-19 had ever been mentioned!

**Kevin Jones** has written many, many stories for the horror world and contributes a story about nasty little goblins to this Halloween fest.

**Carie Juettner** is a middle school teacher and the author of *The Ghostly Tales of New England* and *The Ghostly Tales of Austin*. Her poems and short stories have appeared in publications such as *Tales to Terrify*, *Havok*, and *Daily Science Fiction*. Carie lives in Austin, Texas, with her husband and pets. To learn more about her, visit cariejuettner.com.

**Daniel L. Naden** has been a writer for as long as he can remember. His stories explore the irony in life, through the lens of horror, suspense, & sci-fi. His writing has appeared in great anthologies, like: **The Best of Horror Library: Volumes 1-5, The Horror Library: Volume 2, Dark Distortions: Volume 1**, and **Our Shadows Speak**. Dan's latest novella, **Parting Shot** is available from **HellBound Books**, and his short story, *Last Word*, appears in the revenge anthology, **Dig Two Graves, Volume 1**, from Death's Head Press. Dan lives with his wife in Olathe, Kansas.

**Wendy Lynn Newton** is an Australian fiction and non-fiction writer. She is the author of two non-fiction books, and her short stories and feature articles have appeared in many key international and Australian literary and media publications. Wendy is a Full Member of the Australian Society of Authors and spent several years as a member of Write Response, a team of independent Tasmanian arts reviewers, after being selected by Arts Tasmania for an arts@work mentorship. She is currently working on a young adult science fiction trilogy and lives in northern Tasmania with two out-of-control Chihuahuas and two indifferent cats.

wendy.newton.launceston@gmail.com
Instagram: @wendynewtonlaunceston

**Lena Ng** roams the dimensions Toronto, Ontario, and is a monster-hunting member of the Horror Writers Association. She has curiosities published in sixty tomes including *Amazing Stories* and the anthology *We Shall Be Monsters*, which was a finalist for the 2019 Prix Aurora Award. *Under an Autumn Moon* is her short story collection. She is currently seeking a publisher for her novel, *Darkness Beckons*, a Gothic romance.

**Chris Rodriguez** has retired from the horrors of conventional life. She now lives on the brink of inspiration in a 100-year-old cottage in Pocatello, Idaho. Her works have appeared in various themed anthologies including Rhetoric Askew, several by Horrified Press/Thirteen O'Clock, Left Hand Publisher's, *Mindscapes Unimagined*, ParABnormal Magazine, DL Russell's *Nobody Goes Out Anymore* and Blunder Woman Productions, *Wrong Turn*, which has recently won Best Audiobook Anthology at the SOVAS Awards. You can find her latest at https://www.chrisrodriguez-onthebrink.com or https://www.amazon.com/author/chrisrodriguez-onthebrink.

**Rie Sheridan Rose** multitasks. A lot. Her short stories appear in numerous anthologies, including Killing It Softly Vol. 1 & 2, Hides the Dark Tower, Dark Divinations, and On Fire. She

186

has authored twelve novels, six poetry chapbooks, and lyrics for dozens of songs. She is also editor-in-chief for Mocha Memoirs Press and editor for the Thirteen O' Clock imprint of Horrified Press. She tweets as @RieSheridanRose.

**David Turnbull** is a member of the Clockhouse London group of genre writers. He writes mainly short fiction and has had numerous short stories published in magazines and anthologies. His stories have previously been featured at Liars League London events and read at other live events such as Solstice Shorts and Virtual Futures. He was born in Scotland, but now lives in the Catford area of London. He can be found at **www.**tumsh.co.uk.

**Wondra Vanian** is an American living in the United Kingdom with her Welsh husband and their army of fur babies. A writer first, Wondra is also an avid gamer, photographer, cinephile and blogger. She has music in her blood, sleeps with the lights on and has been known to dance naked in the moonlight.

Wondra was a Top-Ten finisher in the 2017, 2018, 2019 and 2020 Preditors and Editors Reader's Poll, including the Best Author category. Her story, "Halloween Night," was named a Notable Contender for the Bristol Short Story Prize in 2015. She can be contacted through her website: https://www.wondravanian.com/.

**Dona Fox** writes short stories and poetry, mainly horror and dark mysteries infused with bits of science fiction. Coming from the Pacific edge of the United States, specters from the Northwest's rainforests, Portland's bridges & Seattle's mean streets often creep into her dark tales.